978-0-6488983-7-5 (ebook)

978-0-6488983-5-1 (paperback)

❀ Created with Vellum

DYED AND BURIED

LIVIA DAY

DYED AND BURIED

LIVIA DAY

1

THERE'S NOTHING QUITE LIKE DRIVING DOWN INTO THE Huon Valley. The dips and bends open up into a welcome view of green and wet, even when the weather is warm and dry everywhere else. From Kingston Beach, it takes around half hour to get yourself thoroughly lost in winding roads of farms and weatherboard huts, some of them still held together with hope and string.

So much of the Huon is up-and-coming now, with a vineyard around every corner and organic cherry farms replacing the older family apple orchards. Five-star restaurants, coffee pop-ups and sushi kitchens are dotted around towns that used to have nothing but a basic takeaway shop and, if you were very lucky, a bakery that did a good custard tart.

It's particularly green and lush at this end of the year (emerging from the frosts and fog of winter, still a few months before bushfire season begins). When I was a wedding planner, we did good business around the Huon. Rustic paddocks for trendy wedding photos, darling traditional churches, mountain views, wineries willing to host a sit-down for eighty people...

Today, I had a different mission.

The house was a new build, high on one of the green hills surrounding the town of Huonville. I assumed that the locals hated it, because it was one of those architectural marvels that looked great in a magazine, but stuck out like a sore thumb in an area where the preferred aesthetic was practical and down to earth. The sun hit the windows as I drove up the gravel driveway; so much glass and shining stainless steel that I lost all vision for several seconds and had imprints blazed on to my retinas.

A thin, impatient looking blonde woman in a killer black dress came out on the steps as I parked my boss's Prius. She shielded her eyes against the sun, looking annoyed at its very existence. A jolt of familiarity went through me. Jeena Harding. She was exactly my age; I went to school with her. Neither of us had been expecting to see each other today. So, this was going to be fun.

"Samantha Sullivan," she said, blinking at me as I got out of the car. "What on earth are you doing here?"

"Diana sent me," I said. I was wearing my oldest jeans and a jumper that had seen better days. If I've learned anything in the last few months, it's how to appreciate garments with staying power. "I'm from Fashionably Late?"

"Oh." I saw Jeena recalibrate what she thought that she knew about me. Then she smiled in a way that was entirely lacking in *nice*. Her manicure clenched down around a shining black tablet, brand-new. "Bit of a comedown for you, isn't it? Grubbing around in other people's cast-offs?"

"There are worse jobs." I wasn't going to say 'better than nothing' because the truth was, the second chance that Diana gave me with Fashionably Late was better than I could have hoped for. I'd fallen on my feet with this job, and I wasn't going to diss it just to make Jeena freaking Harding feel better about herself.

She frowned. "I was promised discretion. I didn't think they'd send someone I know."

"I mean —" I spread my hands wide. Tasmania, mate. Tripping over a person you were at school with every time you try something new is pretty much par for the course.

"Fine." She turned and led the way up her shining white steps, stomping in dress heels that probably cost more than my car. (They wouldn't last long if she treated them like that, my inner Diana informed me. The re-sell value would drop like a rock. But I wasn't here to buy her shoes.)

In the foyer — because yes, this house was big and fancy enough to have its own foyer — a woman in a neat apron hurried over to consult Jeena on some details about appetisers, calling her 'Mrs Harding-Brady.' That was a shocker.

Well, no. No, it wasn't. Donovan Brady was the best looking boy in our year. Of course he ended up married to Jeena Harding, who was so pretty and confident she did part-time modelling during Grade 10.

I remembered how often in our shared art class she would scoff about whatever it was we were working on, because she knew *professional photographers*.

Today, I watched her make a quick series of decisions about spring rolls and sashimi. The second she was done,

Jeena started walking again, expecting me to follow at her heels like a faithful dog. There were a lot of stairs ahead of me: the house was three storeys, built into the side of the cliff. So much glass. So much stainless steel. You wouldn't want to slip on a banana peel on the top floor, that was for sure.

"You never met my husband, did you?" Jeena said as we began our long march upwards.

"I mean, he was at school with us," I replied. Which was probably better than saying 'we never shared a conversation but once had a sexually charged moment in the library involving far too much eye contact.'

She rolled her eyes at me over her shoulder, quite a feat of engineering.

"Not Donovan, god. Who'd marry him? I meant his brother, Ethan. Four years older."

Oh, right. Not totally living the local cliche of meeting your true love in high school, then.

As we climbed the stairs, we passed a series of professional glamour shots that looked like they belonged to a Hollywood life: the engagement party, the wedding, the exotic honeymoon, all the other expensive holidays that followed.

Donovan's older brother was lighter-haired and more clean-cut than I remembered from our high school rebel without a cause, but equally handsome.

"Congratulations," I said awkwardly.

Jeena gave me a startled look over her shoulder, and laughed suddenly, like she'd been wanting to all day. "Weird choice of platitudes, but okay."

I stared blankly at her. I used to be good at this. Being

polite to clients. Knowing exactly what to say in a given circumstance. But the last couple of years drained that out of me. Now I'm lucky if I remember to say 'good afternoon' instead of 'good morning' when sending an email after lunch.

Jeena took pity on me with another toss of her perfect blonde hair. "You know this is an estate sale, right?" she said as she trip-trapped higher up the stairs.

Well, yes, obviously. Oh. *Oh.*

"Your husband died?" I blurted out, scrambling after her like a hapless baby goat. "I'm so sorry. I thought — from the message I thought it was like, an elderly great-aunt or something. That's usually how it goes."

Four years older than us. He hadn't even made it to 35.

"Funeral's this afternoon," said Jeena, head held high. She had recovered her bitchy poise, but now I was feeling a whole lot less judgy about it. Let her have all the emotional armour she wanted. How was she old enough to be a widow? How was I old enough to have gone to school with someone who had to hold a funeral for her husband?

"I'm so sorry for your loss," I managed, more heartfelt than before.

Jeena shrugged, looking cool and brittle. "It is what it is. Here we are. Now." At the top of the last flight of stairs, she stopped short in front of a large metal door, scrolled rapidly through her tablet, then thrust it at me. "Your boss said you'd sign this."

I'd gone along with Diana to countless estate sales over the last few months, learning the trade. I'd never been handed an NDA before. "Mind if I read this?"

"Be my guest."

It was fairly simple; a two page document detailing in fancy legal language that I would not disclose the details of the sale, or the origin of the items, to anyone. Or they'd sue the pants off me. Joke was on them; I had nothing left to lose.

I signed it with a squiggle of my finger and handed the tablet back. "If there's a genie in a lamp in this room, I should warn you, we don't do brasswork."

Oh, jokes. Exactly what a woman wanted to hear on the morning of her husband's funeral. Nice one, Sam.

Jeena unlocked the door. "I want these gone before guests start arriving. You have three hours. Sooner would be preferred."

I stepped around a stack of moving boxes, still flattened, and into... well. A fairy freaking wonderland of wedding dresses.

My first thought was this was the most elaborate practical joke anyone had ever bothered to play on me. Jeena Harding had to be holding some kind of longterm grudge. Why else would she set this up? Wedding dresses, of all things. A cruel reminder of the business I had poured my heart into, and the disaster that left a trail of wreckage through my family *and* many others.

I wasn't over it.

Jeena didn't look delighted with herself, though. So, I guess it was a horrible coincidence, and not a mean girl prank. She stood there, arms crossed tightly over that killer black dress, her head turned away like she didn't even want to look at the room full of bridal wear. "Your boss said you'd pay cash," she said flatly.

I was well aware of the packet of money burning a

hole in my handbag; literally, as the handbag was on its last legs, and the lining was torn in two places. "Diana only gave me two grand. These could be worth that *each*."

They were gorgeous. Airy garments of beauty, power and swagger. Satin and beading and lace. They looked like they'd just walked off the pages of a fashion magazine on the backs of supermodels.

They also, against the odds, looked comfortable. Like a bride could dance the night away and eat a sandwich at the same time. Classy.

"They don't have labels," said Jeena, still sharp as nails. "I'll take the two thousand if you get these out of here, right now. Discreetly. And I never hear about them ever again."

I stepped closer, peering at one of the dresses. "The quality of stitching is excellent. We don't really do wedding dresses, but formal season is coming up. Most of these will end up dyed magenta and sold off to teenagers."

Jeena didn't flinch. Whatever her emotional hangup was about her room full of wedding dresses (seriously, who has a room full of wedding dresses?), she had no love for them. "Perfect," she said, holding out her hand.

I opened my handbag, rummaged around and handed her the fat envelope.

Jeena turned on her heel, as if she couldn't stand to be in the room a moment longer. She didn't even count the stack of golden fifty dollar notes. "Pack them up before you leave. If anyone sees even an inch of white satin sticking out of a box on your way out, my lawyer will be in touch."

So. That's how my day was going so far.

2

I KNOW WEDDING DRESSES. WHEN I STARTED AT
Fashionably Late, pretty much the only fashion I knew
anything about was bridalwear. Not only the big white
frocks themselves (star of the show), but tuxes, matron of
honour hats, cummerbund colours, flower girl options. I
couldn't sew a straight hem to save my life, but I could
spot the difference between ivory and white satin embroi-
dery thread at fifty paces.

When Diana Wave, the most glamorous woman I'd
ever met my my life, glanced at my brutally short resume
and said the magical words 'You're hired — and by the
way, we don't do weddings,' I felt like I'd been rescued
from a burning house.

Her daughter Morgaine, who spends far more time at
the shop counter than Diana, later explained: it wasn't that
they physically prevented brides from buying our frocks
off the racks. But the official policy was purchase only.
Fashionably Late didn't do event consultation, or set up
shopping parties with glasses of champagne. We don't

offer free delivery to weddings, or advertise discounts to wedding planners and bridal conventions. No special treatment means that only the most chill and low-key brides find their way to our tiny shop.

Morgaine later added that the policy is mostly because Diana loves colour and hates to see a whole corner of the shop devoted to 'boring, bland, pointless white.'

And yet, and yet. Here I was, packing fifteen high quality wedding dresses into plain cardboard boxes. A sea of ecru, champagne, ivory and pearl.

I hadn't been kidding about the dye. These were good, natural fabrics. They'd take colour beautifully. And that was my favourite part about working for Diana Wave. Very few garments we took in looked exactly the same by the time we had them out on sale.

(When I was a teenager I always wanted to be the sort of cool individual who made her own clothes, but I didn't know anyone who could teach me, and then… well, my twenties were all about running my own business and making bad decisions about which man to marry. Now at thirty, I finally had a chance to live my dream.)

I finished the packing, and made my way down the massive staircase feeling like a burglar. It took four trips because the boxes were big, and I didn't fancy falling on to those hard marble tiles.

When I die, let it not be bleeding into a broken cardboard box full of wedding dresses.

I didn't see Jeena as I continued my up-and-down relationship with her dramatic staircase. Every now and then I saw a darting face or foot of the busy catering staff, but that was all.

Finally, as I closed the boot on the last of the boxes, an enormous black SUV whooshed past me, sending gravel flying. Rude! I was lucky not to end up with gravel embedded in my paintwork. The black SUV had a personalised license plate (GAV 001), and apart from the colour was identical to a navy blue SUV (GAV 003) already parked.

The driver was a big, older man in an expensive suit. He shouldered his way into Jeena's house like he owned the place. Maybe he did. I was only assuming this was the house where she'd lived with her husband.

I stared at the car for a minute, trying to figure out what felt off about it, and then I twigged. Apart from the clatter of gravel, it had made no sound as it came up the drive. Electric, I reckoned.

I hovered for a moment and then made my way back in to give Jeena the nod that I was done. When I saw her, she was cornered in the lobby being shouted at by the man in the suit. The look on her face was intensely neutral rather than scared, and it wasn't like she was alone in the house. I caught her eye, wondering if she needed saving.

She waved me off, looking if possible even more bored and annoyed at my presence than before.

Right, then. Off I went. With fifteen high-end wedding dresses stashed in my boot.

Kingston Beach is a small suburb: one row of houses and shops in front of a very nice stretch of sand, and a few blocks of similar beachy houses between that and the golf course, plus a street or two built into the hillside, over-looking the view. This spot used to be shack central for the city of Hobart, decades ago when a modest second home for weekends and holidays wasn't an outrageous expression of wealth. These days, even the most shabby and run down houses in this area are barely affordable, though some older residents have managed to hold on.

There's a quirkiness to these streets that you don't get in newer areas. No house or garden are the same. Every now and then, someone slides in to demolish or refurbish one of the original creaky old weatherboard cottages, adding their own aesthetic to the melting pot.

It's a good beach, and close enough to the city that we're never short on foot traffic. There are five of us along the main retail strip: the fish-and-chips (takeaway), the gift shop, the fish-and-chips (sit down, fancy), the coffee/juice bar and, once you've walked past all that, Fashionably Late. In the other direction, on the far side of the road facing the beach, there's a pub surrounded by a sprawling beer garden.

Here at Fashionably Late, we're a — wait, let me get the phrasing right. Pre-loved and upcycled fashion boutique. Unlike the others in our strip, we weren't originally intended as a shopfront. Diana Wave converted a cottage twenty-five years ago, long before the term 'upcycle' was in common usage. Back then, I think the tagline of the shop was 'vintage fashion for modern life.'

We have a showcase shop room at the front with a big window, a sewing studio at the back, the world's tiniest kitchen and an outdoor loo and laundry.

Diana herself barely sets foot in the shop these days.

She claims to be retired, swanning around her magazine spread home, wearing silk kimonos. I have no idea how old she is — she looks like a glamorous fifty-something, but claims she was a shop girl in Swinging Sixties Carnaby Street, which would make her… well. Possibly a vampire, definitely over 70. She still co-ordinates most of the purchasing, especially the estate sales. So only slightly retired.

In the shop we have Diana's daughter Morgaine, and her apprentice Paisley. They do most of the hands-on stuff, all the ripping of seams and renovating garments to be new, beautiful works of art you can wear.

Then there's me, Sam the dogsbody. I do what I'm told. As the newest employee that means a bit of every-thing, mostly washing new stock and fabrics (so much laundry!), minding the till, and telling people how great they look in their fabulous new frocks. Today's pick-up job was one of those 'no one else wants to go for a drive' tasks that often comes my way.

I love it. After running my own business (and, towards the end, being crashed and burned by my own business), there's a delicious freedom in being paid by the hour and not having to make any of the crucial decisions.

Plus, sometimes, they let me dye.

Morgaine's ex is a builder who specialises in renovations — good business around here, with so many older homes needing work, newer homes that apparently need to be renovated every 3-5 years, and skyrocketing house prices thanks to mainlanders coming over here and nicking our real estate. The Fashionably Late cottage has a long thin yard out the back, so Morgaine's ex built her a laundry shed that runs the whole length of it. There's a couple of washing machines and a dryer for the wet winters, plus a selection of old bathtubs pulled out of various other houses over the years, which we use for the dyeing. There's a covered verandah for long tea breaks, and two Hills Hoist washing lines.

On this particular day, I was making green.

Green was the on-trend colour for formalwear that year, thanks to a few infamous red carpet appearances, and the preferences of a couple of reality TV stars that I could never quite remember the name of. There had been a hugely popular punk rock adaptation of *A Midsummer Night's Dream* in all the cinemas a couple of months back, featuring Aussie pop star Colette Cray as Puck. Morgaine rightly guessed that 'fairy forest' fashion was going to be big. We'd already had a few big-eyed teens in ripped tights scoping out the shop in the hope we could make them look like Titania or Peaseblossom.

Morgaine had laid in huge swathes of ivy lace and cobwebby satin for the months ahead. She and Paisley had been making silk flowers for weeks. We already had several dresses in the window that looked like they'd escaped from a magical woodland, paired with fishnet gloves and hand-painted canvas boots.

Now I'd scored this batch of blank canvases, we'd have all we needed for formal season.

Not all of Jeena's wedding dresses would be repurposed for the store — of the fifteen I bought, five were too delicate, too beaded, too extravagantly layered in good quality lace. Diana had made off with those after the briefest of inspections when I first returned from the Huon with my boxes full of flounce. She'd probably resold them already, shipping them off to her other daughter who ran the kind of bridal shop where they charged a fortune per frock and served French champagne in the dressing rooms.

I loved working with bright colours — there was a purple mini-dress hanging in the shop that used to be a very drab beige, one of my proudest recent achievements. Morgaine was pushing for Fashionably Late to go 100% environmentally sustainable when it came to our dyes and materials (we were currently hovering at about 80% and climbing). That often meant allowing for a softer colour — more sage green than kelly green, if you know what I mean — but the effects could be lovely. Especially when you had white fabric to start with.

You can make natural green dyes from lots of things — artichokes, chamomile leaves, foxglove and nettle. Even good old fashioned grass. Today's concoction was extracted from dandelion stalks and spinach leaves, cut and soaked for days, with alum as the mordant (fixative) to turn the soup into a dye instead of a very unpleasant tasting tea.

It's tricky, though, green. Starting with the whitest of white is the best way to get a good result.

I started with a t-shirt, to test the colour of this batch. It came out a little paler than I'd expected, but came up much more intensely on a swatch of silk. Then I started on the gowns — three of them were now fully coloured, one with only the hem dip-dyed in green, hanging wetly on the Hills Hoist.

Morgaine came around to check my work. "Not bad," she said, examine the fabric minutely. "Maybe something more dramatic for the next batch?" She pulled out a few tins from the topmost shelf that looked more vintage than any gown we had hanging in the shop. "Add some purple to a second bath for layering. And a few drops of this to get a stronger emerald."

It was a good morning's work. By the end of it, I had filled the Hills Hoist with green and purple gowns in various shades. No streaks on any of them. Perfect.

"It was a lucky find, this lot," Morgaine said, nodding with satisfaction as she surveyed the laden washing line. "All good fabrics." Chiffon and fine hemp, plus several in real silk. I'd never worked with such lovely stuff.

"They took the colour well," I agreed. "Anything else you want green or purple before I drain off the baths?

"Hang on," she said, popping inside. "I have a few metres of tulle that needs pepping up. And some organic cotton."

"Fine, but I draw the line at your socks!" I called after her.

"Yeah, yeah. I'll have you doing blues next. I think you're ready to level up."

It was quite a thing, to achieve competence at something new, after recovering from the worst disaster of my life. Worthy of a celebratory cup of tea and a biscuit.

I was sitting on the verandah in the sunshine, about to bite into a well-deserved Scotch Finger, when I heard Paisley calling to me from the back door of the shop.

Paisley is nineteen and non-binary (pronouns: they/them). Everything from their clothes to their friends to their music is just so — I feel like a dag if I say 'cool,' but honestly. When I was their age, I didn't know anyone as put together as Paisley's generation of teenagers. They all seem to know who they are, what they want, where they're going, and exactly what they feel about gendered expectations.

Morgaine might be the expert dressmaker, but Paisley can take a few scrappy old shirts and transform them into pure art. They have ten times more confidence than I have.

Today, lounging on the back step in floral denims and a tailored stripey shirt, Paisley looked like they had just walked off an Instagram page.

"Oi, Sam!" they called to me. "Police want a word with you."

And suddenly the day went cold around me. Last time the police wanted a word with me, my world fell apart.

I stood up, awkward, not knowing what to do with the biscuit still clutched in my hand. Paisley ducked back inside, obviously not realising anything was wrong. A moment later, Donovan freaking Brady strode through the back door of the shop, all black suit and giant mirrored shades like he was working for the CIA, not the local cops. I hadn't thought of him in years, not until yesterday when I found out Jeena Harding was his sister-in-law.

"Excuse me," he said, all business as he turned his gleaming sunglasses in my direction. "Are you Samantha Sullivan?"

I stared back at him, blinking like an idiot at the man who had once been the hottest boy at my high school. My initial shock at those words — at the idea of the police stomping into my life all over again and exposing all the cracks I hadn't known existed — faded into something else.

Pure indignation. Because yeah, it was a long time since high school. We'd all changed since then. But did he seriously not remember me at all? I was going by my maiden name again. I practically still had the same hair style.

"Yes. What do you want?" I asked, managing to keep my voice even.

"I'm investigating the whereabouts of a shipment of valuable wedding dresses," he said, in an official tone of voice, just a slight air of thread hanging on to his words. "Missing from their owner's house, presumed stolen. Know anything about that, do you?"

With my heart frozen in my chest, I could not stop my eyes shifting to the Hills Hoist where so many wet gowns were hanging in their various shades of sage green, mint green, emerald and violet, flapping in the spring breeze.

3

DONOVAN BRADY, POLICE OFFICER, FOLLOWED MY GAZE.
For a moment we both stared at the wet, dyed dresses
hanging on the Hills Hoists. They'd look spectacular when
they were dry. One of them, my favourite, was made of a
sort of fluffy chiffon crepe in scooped layers, so that it
frothed out delicately. I'd dipped it in green early on in the
day and left the underneath layer white so it could be dyed
purple later. Someone was going to feel like a mermaid
princess at her high school leaver's event.

I felt sick. All that white silk. Worth a fortune. And I'd
known — I'd *known* it was too good to be true.

"What do you mean stolen?" I managed. "We paid for
the dresses. As arranged by my boss."

Slowly, the police officer took off his huge mirrored
sunglasses. Donovan must have been seventeen or so, last
time I saw him, and we were both around thirty now. He'd
grown up from a stupidly good-looking teenager into a
steady adult with dark eyes and a good jawline.

It didn't make him any less terrifying.

"Are those really —" he said, and swallowed, looking horrified. "Shit. What did you do to them?"

Now I was all the way back to annoyed. Talk about an emotional rollercoaster. "It's *on trend*," I snapped at him. "I told her we'd be dyeing them for the high school formals, and she didn't care. No one stole anything."

"How much did you pay for them?" he demanded. "Was this Jeena's idea?"

I was starting to get suspicious. "Are you really a police officer?"

"Who told you I was a police officer?" he asked, sounding genuinely surprised.

I let out a deep breath. Bloody Paisley, making assumptions. Couldn't kids today tell the difference between a genuine authority figure and some rando off the street in a pair of giant sunnies?

"If you're not a police officer, or like, the *fashion police*, why should I answer your questions?" It was a fair question, and I was feeling cranky as I asked it.

Donovan Brady turned his officious smoulder on to me. I stood firm against it, refusing to be impressed. I'd done enough girly swooning over him when I was fifteen. "I represent *Impeccable Magazine*."

Well, that required a whole different kind of swooning. *Impeccable* was one of the most successful fashion magazines in Australia, fighting against the tide of free content on the internet by charging like a wounded bull for their glossy pages, and claiming the title 'prestige' into the bargain. It's scary how many women enjoy more than being told to raise their personal expectations from fancy to impossibly perfect.

What I wanted to do was to quiz Donovan on what choices you had to make in life to end up working for *Impeccable Magazine*. Instead, I concentrated on looking as unimpressed as possible. That's what Diana Wave would do, and I often call up my inner Diana in times of stress. "So?"

"So," he said, continuing to smoulder at me in what could only be called an antagonistic manner. "Those dresses were contracted for a photo shoot that is scheduled to happen this weekend. The designer was paid ten grand for exclusive access to the collection. My company has responsibility for the security of the shoot, including collection and delivery of the original wedding dresses between the designer's agent, and the on-site team. Also, as wedding dresses, *they are all supposed to be white*."

He was building up a good head of righteous fury. Now was probably not the time to explain to him the difference between white, ivory and ecru. I could concede that 'not green and purple' was enough of a definition of white for now.

I should be panicking. Everything inside my body was screaming out to apologise and explain. But... actually. The best thing about working for someone else is that when something this huge happens to the business, it's not your responsibility.

Also, he wasn't the police. Fashion or otherwise.

"I don't know what to tell you," I said calmly. "The dresses were bought in good faith by Diana Wave on behalf of Fashionably Late."

"From Jeena Harding-Brady," sighed Donovan. He

looked defeated. I might feel sorry for him, if he'd bothered to remember me from high school.

"I'm pretty sure I shouldn't even have told you this much. Client confidentiality and all that. Also, I signed an NDA."

"There's ten dresses hanging on that line behind you," he said finally. "Do you have the rest?"

I should have shut my mouth. But he now looked a lot more miserable than threatening, and I've always been a sucker for sad eyes on a handsome man.

"You'd need to ask Diana," I said reluctantly.

"Do you think she'd be willing to talk to me? As soon as possible?"

Luckily for him, he was a handsome man in a good suit, and that was Diana's type. "I think she'll be able to squeeze you into her schedule."

Morgaine was happy to let me leave half an hour early to introduce Donovan to Diana. Visiting her mother always counted as a legit work activity, and she pushed a few garment boxes and sketchbooks into my arms before I left, to remind me that I was still on the clock.

When I mentioned Donovan was trying to track down the dresses that his sister-in-law sold us, Morgaine's frown curved all the way deep into her face. "I knew there was something off about that contract. Diana will have to deal with it."

I couldn't imagine a relationship where I called my

mother by her first name, but Morgaine and Diana were
something else.

"You'll hang the dresses inside before you leave for the
night?" I checked. My first big batch of gown dyeing, and
this had to happen. I knew that as far as Donovan was
concerned, the dresses were ruined, but until ten minutes
ago I had been so proud of the work I'd done.

Morgaine looked sympathetic. "Don't let him rattle
you. They look fabulous. Of course I'll take care of them."

"It's not far," I told Donovan as he made to cross the road
towards an enormous SUV. It looked a lot like the one that
had chewed up the gravel at Jeena's house, though this one
was green and the license plate said GAV-002. I guess the
family had an endless supply of super expensive electric
four-wheel-drives. Must be nice. "We can walk."

He hesitated, and then nodded.

We walked along the wide pavement in silence apart
from the crashing waves of the beach. It's a popular beach,
with high rocky cliffs at each of the far ends, and usually
full of people. Cars are always parked in one thick ribbon
facing out to sea, even on rainy days. If I was walking with
anyone else I'd suggest we cross the road to get the nice
ocean view as we went, but Donovan had been deliberately
trying to scare me. He didn't deserve a nice view.

I wanted to know a lot more about what he was after,
but I was fairly certain he wouldn't take my questions seriously. That didn't matter, because I had a secret weapon up
my sleeve.

I had Diana Wave.

~

Kingston Beach is just another example of white colonists deciding to recreate British traditions halfway across the world. Tasmania is full of that sort of thing. Random Scottish castles rebuilt brick by brick. Celtic knotwork on churches. Rose gardens and gorse bushes. The bumblebee.

This particular little corner of the world — the beach and the six blocks of shabby suburbia behind the beach — was designed for holiday escapes, a touch of affordable luxury. Which, in the 50s when a lot of these houses were built, was not about subtlety. The streets are all named after British royalty, for a start. Victoria, Albert, Windsor, Balmoral.

Speaking of England and their royal family, the first thing you need to know about Diana Wave is that after she settled here in the late 70s, she was mildly obsessed with Arthurian mythology, and so she named her daughters Morgaine and Viviane.

(I say settled, but from all the stories she tells, she didn't spend a lot of time stuck in Tasmania over the decades. She was following rock bands around New York, managing catwalk shows in London, running an arthouse cinema in Sydney. It all sounds like bullshit, and to be honest I assumed that for the longest time, but every now and then she runs into some old mate of hers and they corroborate everything. Her Wikipedia page is a bizarre joy.)

Diana's house is the last one on the beach road, with a

clear view of the gorgeous grey-blue waters of the wide Derwent River. Yes, it's not technically the sea, but the water is salty and this estuary is tidal enough that there's little point in quibbling about it. If it looks like a beach and smells like a beach...

In keeping with the mix-and-match style of this suburb, Diana's place is a palatial Art Deco two storey house, with rounded corners, slotted windows and bright white paintwork. Not a live plant in sight; what little front garden she has was covered in quartz pebbles years ago.

She has those old-fashioned metal house numbers stuck up on the outer wall, as well as the name of the house in bold, moulded cursive writing: Avalon.

"Really?" said Donovan skeptically.

I rolled my eyes at him and rang the doorbell.

"Samantha, darling!" Diana Wave appeared on her threshold, draped in a bright red Moroccan tunic with soft silk trousers. Her dark hair as usual was cut sharply, an asymmetrical bob that made her look like she'd wandered out of a Parisian cafe. "I was just thinking about you. Let's have coffee."

Diana hates the outdoors; all her gardening magic is performed on indoor plants. Donovan and I made our way through a jungle of hanging ferns and other leafy tropical greens towards her sunroom at the back of the house, where she prefers to entertain.

Knowing my role, I made straight for the kitchen and put the electric jug on, assembling the coffee pot and cups on a tray. Diana has a nice lady called Maisie who pops in to help with 'little things' three days a week but this wasn't one of her days. I felt no guilt at all about throwing

Donovan to the wolves, so to speak. Let him introduce himself.

"But of course I know your father," Diana was saying when I stepped into the bright sunroom. She lounged on her favourite basket chair, surrounded by a halo of soft light breaking through her Japanese paper blinds. She nodded graciously to me as I set down the tray. "Gavin Brady tried to sell me one of those electric tanks to me last year, when I specifically told him I wanted something tiny, for running around town."

Donovan nodded gravely. "He doesn't listen well to what other people need."

"Terrible quality in a salesman, you'd think."

Donovan laughed at that. It was something of a shock, as he'd been so rigid and serious all day. But it made his face light up. "He does all right."

"Successful businessmen are so dull," she sighed. "It's impossible to tell them that they're wrong about anything."

"And are you ever wrong about anything?" he challenged her.

Diana's eyes widened. "Constantly! That's what life is all about."

It was hard to be grumpy at anyone who clearly enjoyed Diana's presence. She was one of my favourite people in the world. Still, we were here for a reason.

"Donovan wants our wedding dresses," I informed Diana, and pushed down on the coffee plunger.

"We don't do weddings," Diana said instantly. "Too much trouble."

"But you took possession of fifteen wedding dresses

yesterday," said Donovan, sounding like a police officer again.

"Bought," I corrected. "We bought the dresses from Jeena Harding-Brady. Legitimately."

"Indeed, we did," said Diana, her expression cooling. She accepted the cup of coffee I handed her: black, with half a teaspoon of sugar, in tiny cups she had bought somewhere near Nice while holidaying with a member of the Royal Family of Monaco. (Yes, I remember all her stories. I love all her stories, even if they remind me that I've been nowhere and done nothing.) "Thank you, darling."

"They were not Jeena's dresses to sell," said Donovan gruffly.

Diana peered at him, unimpressed. "I was under the impression they formed part of a late relative's estate."

I had half forgotten, in all this, that Donovan had recently lost a brother, far too young. It was probably too late to murmur condolences. I was all tensed up, waiting to be blamed for the whole disaster. There was a fleck of green dye on my wrist, from where it had dripped under my glove. It made me feel like Lady Macbeth.

I had taken ten valuable wedding dresses belonging to someone else, and basically murdered them.

Diana regarded Donovan Brady from over the top of her tiny coffee cup. "Why don't you start from the beginning, my dear? I can't help until I know what we're dealing with. Let's start with how exactly you came to work for *Impeccable Magazine*."

Oh, good. I wouldn't need to ask a single question. Diana Wave was on the case.

4

Donovan Brady looked trapped, his large frame crammed into the dainty basket chair, with a tiny coffee cup resting on his knee.

I knew how he felt. I remembered sitting here the first time I visited, desperate to impress this impossibly elegant older woman enough to get the job offer I needed so badly. Somehow, I ended up spilling out my entire messy life story, all over her fancy designer rug. And somehow, impossibly, she hired me anyway.

"How did you know I'm from *Impeccable*?" he asked suspiciously.

There was a point. I hadn't called ahead, as I'm used to dropping in on Diana. She's always ready for guests, as long as we don't have the bad taste to arrive before 10am — and even then she'll welcome you in, wearing her shining silk pyjamas, and drop hints about how you should poach an egg in her general direction.

Morgaine must have given Diana the heads-up. She

gave no indication of this, offering him a lipsticked smile. "I have my ways." She liked to keep people guessing.

"I run Brick Wall, a security and PR company in Sydney," Donovan said, after a long enough pause to accept that Diana was not going to offer anything else. "We have a lot of high profile celebrity clients. *Impeccable Magazine* are new to our list. They still have their own in-house security, but we've been handling events on location. Photo shoots, galas, that sort of thing. We've booked a major wedding shoot this weekend, down the Huon. Rustic backgrounds, hay bales, that sort of thing."

"Hay bales," I said in surprise. "In September? We've just come out of winter."

Donovan closed his eyes, looking pained. "Please don't talk to me about hay bales. I just spent the last fortnight of my life arbitrating disputes between an art director and several farmers about the sourcing of hay bales. Believe me, the hay problem is sorted. The wedding dress problem, however, continues." He shot me a filthy look.

I sipped my coffee. The meaner he was about it, the less guilty I felt about dyeing his frocks green. I had, after all, improved them.

"I'm afraid we can't help," said Diana. "I spoke with Ms Harding-Brady on the phone myself. We exchanged email confirmations and a contract. I did inform her that she would make more money if she sold them directly to a bridal shop, but she was more concerned with getting a cash payment for a quick sale."

"And getting them out of the house before the funeral," I murmured.

Neither of them registered my comment.

"Really," said Diana in a low and chiding tone. "The issue is between yourself and Ms Harding-Brady. We bought the items in good faith, and I have an email receipt that she sent me shortly after Samantha here picked up the merchandise."

"Jeena didn't own the dresses," Donovan insisted. "Ethan didn't even own them. I don't know what she was thinking, she won't discuss it with me. But my brother was only acting as an agent between the designer and the magazine for exclusive access to the collection."

"That is unfortunate," said Diana crisply. "But there is little we can do about it now. I would happily sell the dresses back to the designer, but I believe they are no longer in their original condition." She glanced at me. "I don't suppose any of them…"

"Green," I said glumly. "Some of them are purple. They look really great."

"But they don't look like wedding dresses any more," said Donovan between gritted teeth.

"I do have some good news on that front," said Diana, rummaging in a fringed black silk purse. She handed over a blindingly white business card. "Some of the gowns weren't quite our sort of thing. A little too bridal to be useful for our current range. I sold them on to a local boutique. If you're quick, you may be able to get part of the collection back."

~

"Well, good luck with that," I said cheerfully as we emerged blinking on to the pavement, surrounded by the sound of crashing waves.

"Oh no," said Donovan, starting to walk in his long stride back along the street. "You're coming with me."

"Why would I do that?"

"Because you know these people. It will save time to have you there."

"It won't save *me* time. I'm done for the day, and I want a bath, not a tour of Hobart's bridal boutiques." AKA the worst possible tour down memory lane I could possibly imagine.

He gave me an impatient look. "You owe me."

"How exactly do I owe you?"

"You dyed my dresses green."

"They're not your dresses," I shot at him. "And I happen to think they look better that way. Newsflash: no one actually looks good in white. That's a lie that magazines like yours tell ordinary women, who end up spending five times the price of a fabulous dress just to look washed out on their big day."

"You have a lot of opinions on wedding dresses," he said, sounding slightly put out.

"Is that supposed to be a joke?" I demanded of him.

Now he just looked confused. "Why would it be a joke?"

I stopped still on the pavement. "You really don't know who I am, do you?"

It was almost refreshing. The trouble with a place like Tasmania is that even in the city, you can't get away from people who know you. And everyone who knew me knew exactly why I have so many opinions on wedding dresses.

Donovan turned to stare at me. "What's that supposed to mean? Are you famous for something?"

"Yes," I said calmly. "I'm famous for going home. Right now. Bye."

His shoulders sagged a little in his good suit. "Please," he said hopefully. "Come along and introduce me to this Vivi woman. The magazine sent me pictures so I'd recognise the dresses, but I still feel like an idiot in those places. I'd probably come back with half the wrong ones."

I had tried to train myself out of being a sucker for a man in a nice suit. This one, at least, was capable of saying 'please' which put him head and shoulders (emphasis on the shoulders) above my ex-husband.

"Fine," I said. "But don't push it. Feeling guilty about my expert dye job will only take us so far in this relationship."

Donovan gave me half a smile which made him look a whole lot more real than when he was glaring. There was still a sadness about his eyes, and I was reminded all over again that this man had just lost his brother. Chasing after a stack of runaway wedding dresses was probably better than dwelling on that.

Bridezillion was exactly what you'd expect from the most expensive bridal boutique in a very small city like Hobart. Acres of white fabric draped over tiny-waisted mannequins.

There's a high turnover with all fashion stores, but especially those with specialised interests. It was 18 months or so since I last had anything to do with the wedding industry, which meant at least half of the local bridal wear stores were new to me.

This one, though. It was Your Special Day two years ago, and Melissa's Bridal two years before that. There's something about this particular dainty retail space in Sandy Bay that calls to businesses hoping to mark up a truckload of ivory frocks in a short space of time.

I knew the owner. Vivi was around my age, and had always been in the wedding industry one way or another: sales assistant, rising to assistant manager, bouncing around the various fashion outlets. When I first met her, years ago and long before her mother became my boss, she was PA to one of my greatest professional rivals, a woman known to her peers as The Wedding Shark because of her extreme ruthlessness in party planning. It was no surprise to me at all that Vivi ended up running a bridal boutique.

"Samantha," she said sweetly as I ushered Donovan into the narrow shop. He did indeed look super awkward, his wide shoulders surrounded by tulle and silk flowers, like a bulldozer in a tea glass emporium. "Feeling nostalgic for the old days?"

"I miss it so," I said in a flat voice. "We need to talk to you about those wedding dresses your mother sold you yesterday."

No one would pick Vivi and Morgaine for sisters, and not only because there's a decade or so between them. Morgaine is all natural fibres and solid frame: no makeup, steady voice and calm practicality. Vivi is a livewire tiny pixie person, blending unadulterated ambition with Insta-perfect makeup.

"Oh, weren't they a find!" she crowed. "I already sourced buyers. Lovely work — I thought I'd struggle to sell them without labels, but you know what brides are like when they find The Dress. Are there more where that came from?"

I introduced Donovan and stood back, still wondering why he thought I was necessary for this excursion.

Donovan went into his practiced spiel — in this version the dresses were sold by accident, but he had enough authority to carry it off.

Vivi, whose ears pricked up the second she heard him namedrop *Impeccable Magazine*, was practically vibrating with excitement when Donovan pulled up images of the dresses on his phone. I peered shamelessly over his shoulder as he hadn't bothered to show these to me before now. Each dress was sketched in pencils, with notes on fabrics and design elements. There was a watermark on each picture which looked like a cartoon lizard.

"OMG," Vivi said, practically hanging over the counter to get a better look. "Is this the new Chameleon collection? Everyone's been dying to see it!"

Donovan's face closed over and he stepped back. "We don't have to…"

"No, let me see! I can't believe I had genuine Chameleon dresses right here and I had no idea. Why weren't the labels on them yet? I could have charged several thousand each for Chameleon wedding dresses. I let the last one go for six fifty!"

"What's the Chameleon collection?" I interrupted.

Donovan slipped his phone back into his pocket.

Vivi looked at me like I was from Mars. "Are you kidding? You really have been out of the game, Sam. Chameleon is the hottest indie designer this year, and no one knows who they are. I'm so glad I took pics of the dresses before I sold them, those are going right on my Insta."

"No social media," Donovan growled. "Those dresses are confidential. If images get out online before the *Impeccable* photo shoot, my bosses will sue anyone who was involved."

Vivi rolled her eyes at him. "Shouldn't have lost them, then, should you?"

She had a point, but I was too busy quietly hyperventilating about being sued to enjoy the moment.

Donovan sighed. "Can you give me contact details for the customers that purchased the dresses? Hopefully they'll be willing to have the magazine hire them back for the shoot, or purchase them outright."

Vivi gave him a sharp look. "I kind of feel like *that* would be a breach of confidentiality."

He leaned in and smouldered a little, clearly used to people just doing what he asked for. "I'd appreciate it very much."

She smirked, smelling blood in the water. "How about a trade? You tell me if the rumours about Chameleon designing a dress for Colette Cray's wedding are true, and I'll tell you who bought the ones I had here."

Even I'd heard of Colette Cray, thanks to her association with the *A Midsummer Night's Dream* fashion craze among teenagers. I looked at Donovan with new eyes. A security firm, he said. Big name clients. Was he really after the dresses for the magazine, or was there something more going on? Something involving a certain pop star actress?

"What rumours?" said Donovan with an expressionless face.

"Hmm," said Vivi. "Do you want me to sell you back the one dress I didn't find a buyer for yet?"

"Yes," he snapped.

"Show me the pics first, prove which one's yours," she said, making a grabby gesture.

He opened his phone and scrolled through more pictures. "This one?"

"Nope, nope, hang on, maybe." She took the phone from him and to my surprise, Donovan let her. "This one, I think. Let me just check!" Phone in hand, she whisked herself into the back room and closed the door.

"You're going to regret that," I remarked.

"Entirely possible," he agreed, rounding the counter and starting type rapidly at Vivi's computer screen, pulling up the contact information for recent sales.

They were clearly as bad as each other.

I decided to wait in the car.

5

THE BIG GREEN ELECTRIC SUV WAS LOCKED, SO I LEANED against it to wait. What on earth was I doing here? Agreeing to help out a man in a nice suit with sad eyes was one thing, but my work day was over, and I wanted to go home.

Finally, Donovan emerged with a zipped garment bag hanging over one shoulder. He unlocked the car, and tossed it into the back seat. "One down. Shall I drop you back to Kingston Beach?"

"Yes please," I said fervently.

We took the Taroona road back, all winding curves, scenic coastal views, and occasionally having to slow down drastically so as not to knock cyclists over the cliff. Donovan was a careful driver, more respectful on the road than I'd have expected, based on how he did everything else.

"How did things go with Vivi?" I asked in the end, burning with curiosity. "Is she going to put the wedding dress photos all over her socials?"

"We came to an agreement," said Donovan calmly. "She'll contact the buyers of the other dresses and explain that I need to talk to them. Give them a chance to get in touch."

"That will probably have better results than you calling them out of the blue with the contact details you nicked off her computer," I guessed.

He shrugged. "Time's short. Doesn't hurt to have back up. I have an art director, three models and a photographer all flying into Hobart tomorrow, and I was hoping to be able to show up to the shoot with more than one dress."

"How did you convince Vivi to go along with it?" I couldn't help asking. She wasn't the most compliant of people.

"Offered to introduce her to Colette Cray," he said with a hint of a smirk.

I laughed out loud. "That would do it."

"Speaking of…" He took his phone out of his pocket, thumbed it open and passed it to me. "You bought sixteen dresses from Jeena, correct?"

"Fifteen."

"Was this one of them? I didn't spot it on that washing line, and Vivi swears it wasn't with her batch."

I looked at the picture. Like the others, it was a fashion sketch in soft pencils with a lizard watermark. I didn't recognise the gown, though — it was nothing like the others. A huge, bell-shaped skirt, frothing out in scoops to knee-length like a retro ballerina, or something out of an Audrey Hepburn movie. There were all kinds of textures and complicated beading patterns I didn't quite under-stand. There were circles all over the skirt that were too big to be beads. Were they holes punched into the fabric? Round feathers? Hand-embroidered rose petals? The gown was paired with the lightest of cobwebby capes with what looked like gauze fairy wings hanging down behind the dress.

This dress, unlike the others, was named. <u>The Titania</u> was scrawled above the sketch in pencilled lettering.

It was gorgeous. It would fit our *Midsummer Night's Dream* window display perfectly except, of course, it was designed to be made up in white, white, white.

Was I looking at a celebrity's wedding dress?

"I've never seen it before."

"That's what Jeena said," Donovan grunted. "She only found fifteen at the house, and sold them all to you."

"And you don't believe her?"

"I don't believe Jeena sold a valuable designer collection to some random op shop without asking any questions about what the dresses were and why they were in Ethan's possession," said Donovan. "Reality doesn't make a lot of sense right now. All I'm doing is trying to clean up the mess."

That 'op shop' crack stung. Not that there's anything wrong with op shops. But we at Fashionably Late are a retro upcycled fashion boutique, thank you very much!

Before I could work up another head of steam, Donovan gave me a sideways smile as he turned off the Taroona Road towards Kingston Beach. "Don't worry about it. I'm sure it can all be fixed by cleverer people than me."

I frowned a bit. Did he… actually think it was possible

to take a green and purple gown and strip it back to the original white?

It was definitely above my pay grade to break that news to him. I gave him directions to where I lived, opposite the duck park.

"I've been handling events for *Impeccable* all year and I still don't get fashion," Donovan confessed as he pulled up in front of my place: a very old fashioned and slightly shabby cottage with pots of geraniums heaped up on the porch. "How can dresses possibly be worth so much money? They're not cars. Surely at some point you run out of ways to jack the price up. Nice spot, this."

"It belongs to my sister's ex-husband's dead auntie," I replied, nonsense but true. "What do you mean, you don't get fashion? You're wearing a great suit."

"Thank you?" he said, sounding a bit wounded, like I'd maybe insulted him.

"I mean. That doesn't happen by accident."

"My brother was the suit guy," he confessed, looking sad again. Those big hound dog eyes of his. "Ethan had this whole thing about — how important it was, in business. Especially in Australia because loads of blokes don't bother with it apart from figuring out when you wear a tie, and when you don't. When I started my company, Ethan flew up to Sydney and took me to like, five different places. Showed me how to pick a suit that makes you look intimidating, or one that makes you fade into the background..."

"And today you picked intimidating."

He laughed. "Dealing with wedding dresses! I know when I'm out of my depth."

"Wedding dresses are always over-priced," I agreed, following on from his previous comment. "Everything in weddings comes with an insane mark up. But fashion is useful for a lot of things. It can be used in professional situations to get a specific result. The right tie, the intimidating suit, the cut of the fabric. For most people, it's about expressing themselves through what they wear. In the case of designer dresses — well, you pay more because if you don't, someone else will. You've buying exclusivity, expertise. A name brand label. And — sometimes you just want to wear a pretty frock for a special occasion and feel amazing."

He shrugged easily, not as invested in the topic as I was. "You know, I grew up around here. Jeena and I went to school up the road."

"You don't say," I said dryly. Seriously. He still didn't remember me? It was a big school, but we had classes together for four freaking years.

"I thought she'd be good for Ethan," he said, shaking his head. "She was always nice around me. But things have been rough with them for a while. She's all — sharp and bitter now. Has been for years."

I was caught horribly between wanting to hear the gossip, and not wanting to be told private information that was none of my business. I also wanted to correct him, because to some of us Jeena had always been sharp and bitter. (She mostly didn't show it around good looking guys, or anyone she wanted to impress... so maybe that transition was less about her marriage being in trouble, and more about her losing interest in what her brother-in-law thought of her.)

I handed back his phone. "It's a beautiful dress. I hope you find it."

"I'd better," he agreed. "Or I'll end up on all the celebrity gossip blogs as that security guy who was kicked in the balls by Colette Cray."

"It's her wedding dress. You're more likely to be shot than kicked. Out of a cannon."

"Weddings make people crazy," Donovan said solemnly. "Wasn't there some other big wedding scandal around here a few years ago? I remember Jeena going on and on about it, thought it was hilarious. Someone from our old school — local wedding planner stole hundreds of thousands of dollars that should have been spent on venues, and ran away to Bali or something. There were all these angry, mascara-dripping brides on the cover of the Mercury…"

"So, I'm going inside," I said sharply. "If you need a sidekick for the rest of your wedding dress adventures, find someone else."

He looked confused as I slammed the car door and headed for the house. But seriously. How did he know my whole sordid story but fail to remember me?

Walking into Aunt Harriet's house is like stepping back in time. I never met her when she was alive, mostly because she devoted her retirement to budget travel around the world, but also because she was not my aunt.

My divorce was a chaos hurricane of drama, trauma, police investigations, lawyers, betrayal and abandonment.

My sister Trace's separation, in contrast, has been almost obnoxiously civilised. They're still figuring things out, all those extra logistics that come into play when there's a kid involved, and shared property, and no pending fraud charges.

She couldn't stand to stay in the family home and couldn't afford to buy something new… and her soon-to-be ex convinced her to let him keep living in the house for their daughter's sake. This was their compromise. A family inheritance that no one had yet got around to doing anything about: Aunt Harriet's fully furnished, rickety old weatherboard house in a Very Good Area. It needs a full reno if it's to be sold anywhere near its value, and neither Trace nor her ex had the energy to tackle it in the two years since Harriet died. So Trace moved in for now and, knowing how ropy my financial situation is these days, she invited me to stay.

It's an odd thing, being the indefinite house guest of a nice dead old lady. Everything in the house is 100% Harriet. She was a quilter and a knitter, which means every surface is layered and cuddly. Even the teapots have jackets. She collected porcelain, so you constantly feel like a sneeze might shatter everything precious in the room.

The books on the shelves are mostly vintage murder mysteries, and reference books to help you build killer cryptic crossword skills, because that's how Aunt Harriet rolled.

The place still smells of her, assuming that her personal scent was dried roses, ginger biscuits and Earl Grey. I've got rather fond of Aunt Harriet. It's like being haunted by a really friendly ghost who wants to make sure I never get chilly.

Trace was home when I let myself in, pottering around the kitchen. "Cuppa?" she yelled out, assuming it was me.

"Yes please!"

My laptop was still on the coffee table where I'd left it that morning. I collapsed on the couch in a sea of throw-cushions, and pulled the laptop towards me. Some serious Googling was in order to fill in some of the gaps from everything weird that had happened to me since Donovan Brady walked into the shop. "So, I spent most of the day trying to solve a wedding dress mystery."

"Oh," Trace laughed from the kitchen. "Your favourite."

"I know, right? I thought Fashionably Late was so perfect for me with Diana's No Wedding policy, and now I'm being stalked by white satin all over again."

My first search choice was 'Colette Cray wedding' and I immediately got a heap of links to recent interviews and articles, all speculating about the pop star's secret fairytale destination wedding which they all, apparently, knew way more about than they should.

Look, I love living in Tasmania. Ours is a gorgeous island state with pretty scenery but when I think celebrity destination wedding, Tassie would not be on my list of likely locations. I guess that was how they had managed to keep it reasonably secret? Though again, *Tasmania*. I don't think anyone's ever successfully kept a secret here for more than five minutes.

(Ugh, if you don't count my husband.)

After scanning a couple of articles, I narrowed the search terms to 'Colette Cray Chameleon'.

Trace wandered out eventually with two mugs of tea, a plate of bikkies and a large cheese and pickle sandwich cut into halves. Best sister. "Can you pick Daisy up from school tomorrow?"

"No worries. I though this was Rich's week?"

"Work trip came up." She wrinkled her nose, and I heroically held myself back from starting the 'he should be paying more child support if he doesn't have her 50-50' conversation that, let's face it, neither of us needed.

"I almost sold a house today," she said, closing her eyes in exhaustion. "Again. I worked with this family for weeks, finally found them the perfect four bedroom in exactly the area they wanted, and they got lured away to the other side of the river at the last minute by you-know-who. Tell me your day was worse."

Ah, the life of a newly licensed Real Estate Agent. Constant hope and heartbreak.

"I murdered ten designer wedding dresses, and I might get sued by a fancy fashion magazine," I told her.

Trace's eyes flew open. "Okay, then. I guess you can have the last chocolate biscuit."

Later, after Daisy was dropped off by her dad and we ate Trace's Macaroni Balls and Mini Quiche Surprise for dinner, I remembered to go back to my detective work.

The internet was extremely excited about Chameleon, an up-and-coming Aussie designer who had managed somehow to stay anonymous despite several active communities existing purely to figure out their identity and location.

Their biggest career triumphs so far included a scarlet suit they'd provided for That Actress From That TV Show to wear when hosting an awards ceremony for female crime writers, and a mini-collection of 'peace silk' bubble dresses that launched online earlier in the year, and sold in a matter of hours via a Melbourne-based influencer called Gordie Mace. And yes, if you searched for 'Colette Cray Chameleon' you came across the huge, undying rumour that Chameleon had been tapped to make the pop star's super secret wedding gown, despite no confirmation from anyone official.

Popular theories included: Chameleon was Gordie Mace, Chameleon was Colette Cray, Chameleon was a New York designer pretending to be Australian, and Chameleon was actually That Actress From That TV Show.

No one was giving any credence at all to the quietly unpopular theory that Chameleon was Tasmanian, or the occasional online hint that Colette Cray's wedding was also happening in Tasmania, because mainlanders like to think nothing cool ever happens here.

I was spending a whole lot of time on something that was none of my business. Rather than quit while I was ahead, I decided to dig one last rabbit hole of curiosity before I put this entire weird day behind me.

Feeling vaguely guilty about it, I Googled to find out what the internet could tell me about the death of Ethan Brady, Donovan's brother.

6

ETHAN BRADY (34) WAS A SALES EXECUTIVE WORKING FOR his father's highly successful car dealership in Hobart, a business credited for the rising popularity in electric cars across Tasmania. Ethan and his wife Jeena Harding-Brady (30) lived in the family home down the Huon (the shiny glass castle on the hillside, I assumed). His father Gavin Brady (59) owned the house (as well as all the family vehicles if those GAV license plates were anything to go by), but lived in an inner-city apartment in Hobart since the death of his wife Cheryl eight years earlier.

Ethan liked to keep fit, and played several sports as well as spending a lot of time at the gym. All the articles about the family (and there were a lot, once you started looking, clearly Gavin Brady was a Big Time businessman, which meant coverage of his son's death across various regional media outlets) liked to emphasise just how sporty Ethan and Gavin both were. Like father, like son.

The tragic twist was that one of Ethan's regular 'keep

fit' exercises was night jogging, along various country roads. He and his father both enjoyed this particular danger sport. They always wore running shoes and shirts with high vis strips, to help cars see them more clearly.

One night, a couple of weeks ago, Ethan was knocked off the side of the highway and down a steep slope, hitting his head on a jutting outcrop of rocks. The pathologist who performed the autopsy presented a report to the coroner suggesting that Ethan died, if not instantly, then very soon after his fall.

The driver who caused the accident had not come forward. There was a preliminary inquest, but not a final coroner's report yet.

By the time I'd read enough articles about Ethan's grieving family, his father's plea for justice and all the sporting medals he won as a small child, I was just about ready to be sympathetic again, not only to Donovan bloody Brady, but to Jeena 'mean girl' Harding-Brady as well.

Presuming, of course, that neither of them had been behind the wheel of the car.

It's possible that other people, normal people, wouldn't immediately leap to that conclusion. But I lost a lot of things when my marriage ended: my career, my reputation, my financial security, my home. And, most of all, my ability to believe that anyone is what they say they are.

Just because I was capable of feeling bad that Donovan Brady had lost his brother did not mean I wanted to see him when I left for work the next morning. But there he was, parked across the road from Aunt Harriet's house, leaning against that big green SUV with two cups of take-away coffee and a hopeful expression on his stupid chis-elled face.

"What can you possibly want from me now?" I burst out.

He looked slightly taken aback, but only slightly. So, he knew he was pushing it. Still, he rallied. "To apologise, for a start."

Well, if it was apology coffee... I crossed the road quickly, snatched the cup off him, crossed back and started walking. I was like, three blocks from the boutique, no reason to climb into what I could only think of as his Enor-mous Profitmobile after reading up on how much money his dad was raking in from selling electric cars to people who wanted to save the planet *and* take up two parking spaces at the same time.

"It takes me four minutes to walk to work," I called behind me. "Better step on it if you want to get the whole apology done in time."

With his long legs, he didn't have to scurry to catch up. Damn him. Another very nice suit. Still from the intimi-dating section of his wardrobe, but you have to admire someone who commits to a look. "I had another talk with Jeena last night. Mostly from outside the bathroom door, because she's still avoiding me."

"I mean, if I'd sold thousands of dollars worth of high fashion that belonged to your employer, I'd hide from you too." I sipped the coffee. It had vanilla in it. I refused to be charmed by that, even if vanilla-flavoured coffee is my third favourite thing in the universe.

"She did, however, mention one detail that made me feel like an idiot."

"Just the one?"

"I didn't realise yesterday that, uh. The wedding planner fraud. That was you. I mean, your husband. I'm sorry."

I kept sipping the coffee because it was the only person in this conversation I was happy with right now. "It's not a time in my life that I like to be reminded about."

"I get that. And I should not have gossiped about you. Especially not, you know. Directly to your face."

"Major social fail," I agreed with him.

"I'm not always good at lightening the mood. In a friendly way."

"I see that about you." He was looking all sad-eyed again, like a puppy in designer tailoring. No one needed to witness that so early in the morning. "Okay, apology accepted. Mostly because of the coffee. Now what do you really want?"

He looked relieved, like he had been dying to get our relationship back on to a businesslike footing, without any of those sticky emotions. "Just a few questions."

"Hit me." We had already turned up leafy Victoria Street, heading towards the beach, and we were picking up speed. Donovan wouldn't have long to ask his questions.

"Are you absolutely sure that the Titania was not among the dresses you collected from Jeena?" He was holding out his phone again.

I took it from him, because I wouldn't mind getting another look at that stunning fashion sketch. "You should be more careful with your phone," I chided him. "You realise Vivi now has copies of all these highly confidential images?"

"I checked," he said dismissively. "She didn't send them to herself."

I rolled my eyes at him. "Either she did, and deleted the messages, or she just used her own phone to take snaps of your screen."

"People do that?"

"I thought you were in security!"

"I'm usually part of a team," he grumbled. "Other people handle the tech side of things."

I stopped, and stared at him. "Phones aren't tech. They're basic human skills."

"Anyway. If you haven't seen this dress in person, it must never have been part of the stash that Jeena sold. She insists it wasn't at the house."

"So it's still with the designer. How do you not have contact details for the designer?"

"No one at the magazine does. Ethan was acting as their agent. He always sounded kind of paranoid, like he thought he'd be cut out of the deal if *Impeccable* had direct access to Chameleon. To be fair, fashion magazines are pretty ruthless."

"But why?" I pressed, getting interested again despite my best intentions. "Why did he care so much? Ethan was rich and successful, working in your dad's business. Why did he care about branching out into the fashion industry?"

"I don't know," said Donovan, looking troubled. "I wish I did. I assumed it was some random opportunity. Maybe he wanted to prove he could be his own success, you know? Instead of just working for our dad."

Something else had been niggling at me. "Did Jeena know about this whole *Impeccable* deal?"

"I can't get a straight answer from her about any of this." He looked at me curiously. "Why do you ask?"

"Because when she handed over the dresses the vibe was all… I don't know, weird. Like she was covering up a dirty secret. She wanted them out of her sight, and she wanted to make sure no one else saw them too."

"I assumed selling the dresses was a random grief thing," said Donovan slowly. "But if she didn't know what they were worth or what Ethan was up to… huh. That is interesting."

I handed his phone back to him. "You need to find Chameleon. The entire internet has tried and failed, but *you* don't do computers, so… maybe if you walk around with old-fashioned detective work, you'll get lucky."

Donovan Brady: Fashion Detective.

"Will you help?"

Damn it, I wanted to. This was the most interesting thing that had happened to me in ages. But I didn't want interesting. I wanted my calm, no stress little job where I got to play with colours and sell refurbished frocks and maybe, at some point, learn to use more than two settings on a sewing machine.

"Nope."

"Can I bounce some ideas off you if I get stuck? You must know the right circles of people. You know fashion and…" He trailed off, clearly realising he was on shaky ground again.

"I used to know the right circles of people. If you mean

the wedding industry in Hobart. But funnily enough, most of them don't talk to me any more."

"I didn't mean —"

We rounded the corner, and I saw a police car parked in the little delivery truck gap between Fashionably Late and the juice/coffee bar. As usual, the very sight of it made my whole body tense up. Top of the list of people I didn't trust? The police. "What's that about?"

My self-preservation instincts were shouting at me to go home and pull a sickie, but… that was my shop. My place. My people.

I braced myself, then strode up the street, ignoring Donovan. He stuck with me as I pushed my way into the shop. The CLOSED sign was still up, as it wasn't quite ten yet. "Morgaine?"

"Back here," she called out.

The two of us squished into the little kitchen, immediately making it too full of people because it already contained Morgaine, Paisley and Sergeant Torrance, one of our local police officers. He was the one who always came around for Neighbourhood Watch meetings, and other community initiatives. I was pretty sure he lived nearby.

Also, he had an embarrassing crush on Morgaine which Paisley was not allowed to tease her about because it made her tetchy.

I could handle Sergeant Torrance, in small doses. I didn't trust him, but I was pretty sure his motivations in coming here were at least 80% non-police related most of the time.

Paisley was sitting on the sink, but with me plus

Donovan and his mighty shoulders, the kitchen was well over capacity.

"What's going on?" I asked nervously.

"Break in last night," said Morgaine. "Smashed a window at the back of the studio. And cut the wires so the security system didn't go off."

"Which is why you need a security system that was installed in this century," Sergeant Torrance reminded her.

"Yes, Arthur, I'll deal with it."

Arthur? Paisley and I locked gazes in equal startlement. We had not been aware that his name was Arthur. I could hear Paisley mentally revising the 'no teasing policy.' Arthurian jokes were always in style around here.

"What was taken?" I asked.

"Oh, no money," said Morgaine, as if it was obvious. "We don't leave anything valuable overnight, you know that."

"But what about the imported silk?" I pressed. "And those Japanese buttons, the really expensive ones."

Morgaine grinned. "I do like your priorities, Sam."

"One of us, one of us," Paisley chanted beneath their breath.

"Were the *Impeccable* dresses taken?" broke Donovan, cutting to the chase.

I saw Sergeant Torrance give him an evaluating look.

Morgaine's friendliness was rapidly waning away. She clearly wasn't a fan of Donovan Brady. "Yes, I've already had your editor blowing up my phone about returning the frocks we legitimately purchased, thank you very much. I've broken it to her that they're not in original state. Either she takes them green and purple or not at all. As it happens, they weren't taken. The intruders didn't think to bust open the laundry shed, and the frocks were hanging up in there to dry overnight."

Sergeant Torrance stood up and faced Donovan with all the officious attitude of a less-than-tall man addressing one who is one twig away from being a giant redwood. "And you are?"

"Donovan Brady, Brick Wall Security." Donovan gave an unthreatening smile which was basically a work of art, and offered a hand to shake. "I'm here to pick up some stray wedding dresses for a magazine shoot."

"Are they valuable, these dresses?" Arthur Torrance asked, glancing back to Morgaine.

"They used to be," Donovan said.

I shot him a dirty look, and took another step closer to Paisley. Sergeant Torrance might be harmless, but I really didn't like him being here.

"Probably someone looking for easy cash," said Morgaine firmly, giving Donovan a much more professional version of a dirty look. "We'll put in a new security system and that will be an end to it. If that's all? I need to open the shop."

It wasn't often that she reminded me of her mother, but Morgaine sweeping both Sergeant Arthur Torrance and Donovan Brady out of the shop in a whoosh of sheer politeness was extremely Diana Wave.

She then returned, looked me squarely in the eye and said "Sam, tell me everything you know about this *Impeccable Magazine* clusterfudge."

Morgaine has been trying to train herself out of swearing, for customer service reasons. Results are mixed.

I dropped my takeaway cup in the bin. "Okay. But it's going to require more coffee."

Morgaine and Paisley are professional problem-solvers. Watching them work on some of the more hopeless vintage garments that end up on our Too Hard Table in the studio is always fascinating to me. They grab a stained slip, or ripped skirt, or horrible colour of upholstered jacket, and they work their magic.

I once watched them take apart a fire-damaged tweed suit, and construct two 1940s-style handbags from the salvaged fabric.

Outlining the situation with the Bradys, the wedding dresses and the mysterious anonymous designer to them both was both helpful and comforting. Mostly because saying all those things aloud reassured me that yes, it had been an odd couple of days.

Morgaine couldn't get over the part where a security professional had let her unreliable sister Vivi make off with his phone for five minutes. "He'd better not have any celebrity pictures on there, or she'll have sold them," she warned.

Paisley was being remarkably quiet. It was Morgaine who asked all the questions.

"What's up?" I asked.

"Do you know about the Swoosh Hutch?" Paisley replied, looking troubled.

"Isn't that where you go for those workshops?" It

sounded vaguely familiar. I had assumed it was a nightclub the first few times Paisley mentioned it.

"Yeah, sometimes. It's a fashion makerspace in West Hobart. A friend of a friend of mine at a party a few months ago told me that everyone local knows Chameleon is totally Tasmanian, and they make their stuff at the Swoosh Hutch."

"Huh."

"You can be fashion detectives after work," Morgaine told us sternly. "Paisley, I need this window tidied. And Sam…"

"Laundry?"

"How did you guess? There's a new bag of denims and cottons in the studio — and I need them thoroughly clean before I figure out what to do with them!"

On it.

At least laundry wasn't going to fill my brains with too many questions and theories. Laundry was just laundry, and right now that was exactly the kind of repetitive task that I needed.

7

THE TROUBLE WITH LAUNDRY WAS IT MEANT SPENDING
time in the laundry shed, being stared at by gorgeous
gowns that weren't supposed to be green and purple.

They looked great. Like, really great. The one where
I'd been brave enough to layer the two colours had come
up so bright and perfectly blended. They were all fabulous.
Chameleon, our mystery designer, had gone for shorter
hemlines all around, no floor-dragging draped skirts,
which provided a party dress air rather than the full
glamour fairy tale. The designs had looked super cute in
white, but they lent themselves beautifully to colour.

The more time I spent with the Frocks That Should Be
White, the crankier I became about the whole disaster.
Whoever was going to end up with custody would probably shove them in a cupboard somewhere as failed
wedding dresses rather than, you know, dresses. Ugh. If I
never saw another white dress again, it would be too soon.

After the laundry it was sales counter time, and then

lunch, and what with one thing and another, the day went fairly quickly.

I was due to leave work to pick up Daisy from school any minute, so I nipped out to take my last batch of washing off the line, before the warmth of the day disappeared entirely and left them all damp. When I came back I found a strange woman leaning on the counter, giving Morgaine a hard time.

The newcomer was short and solid-looking, dressed in those layered linens that look simple but cost a bomb because they flatter any figure. In this case: a soft grey waistcoat over a flowing beige shirt and equally flowing beige trousers. Her hair was tied up in an effortless tangle — the kind that some women can magically manage every time, while others (cough, me) look like they've messed with a flock of magpies if they attempt it.

The woman also had enormous sunglasses that covered most of her face, and spoke in an accent so broadly ocker that you'd think she had walked off the set of an indie film set in the Outback. "Look, sweetheart, I don't care who owns the frocks. I want to photograph them."

"I'm sure you do," said Morgaine, looking calm and amused which was pretty much her default expression. Not much bugged Morgaine. "But I don't work for *Impeccable Magazine*, and I have plans for those dresses. Which I legally own."

Typical. Last I'd heard, Morgaine and Diana were planning to hand the frocks over without any trouble, if the magazine wrote a reasonably compensatory check and didn't complain about the colours. But of course, this woman had put her back up so now she was digging in her heels.

"Morgaine, okay if I leave for the school pick up?" I asked, not wanting to get involved.

Linens stared at me from over the top of her enormous sunglasses. "Are you Samantha Sullivan, by any chance?" she asked directly.

"Nope," I said calmly, and motored on out of there. I had a niece to pick up, and I was done with high fashion melodrama for the day.

Daisy is nine, and one of my favourite people. She's been poring over medical textbooks since before she could read, and shows an almost disturbing fascination with the specific internals of how human bodies work.

Her grandparents bought her the board game Operation last Christmas, and she not only told them that it was anatomically incorrect, but she explained her reasoning at length with diagrams. Many precise, detailed diagrams. It put everyone off their lunch.

Basically, she's going to end up a doctor or a serial killer. Either way, I'm in her corner.

It was that time of afternoon when you have to figure out if you're going to cook a proper tea, or if it's just going to be baked beans on toast all around. Before I could lean one way or the other, Paisley arrived at my door. They had changed since work and wore a light blue jumper with a pattern of plastic spoons arranged in a fan-shaped pattern around the collar (yes, actual plastic spoons sewn on to the jumper).

"Fashion detectives?" I said weakly.

Paisley gave me finger guns, because apparently that was something the younger generation had brought back. "You know it."

"I'm babysitting right now."

"It's not babysitting if it's your child," called Daisy in a sing-song voice from where she was colouring in a hand-made poster in the living room.

"You're not my child," I called.

"Gonna make me cry, Auntie Sam."

Paisley looked past me. "Hi, Dais. Cool snake you're drawing there."

"It's an intestinal tract," said the nine-year-old.

"Cool intestinal tract you're drawing there. I like the textures you're getting with that orange pencil." Paisley glanced at me hopefully. "Swoosh Hutch?"

"Trace won't be home for a couple of hours yet."

"So, bring the kid."

I couldn't think of a reason to say no. "Daisy, do you want to check out a Makerspace? It's like a studio where they have all this equipment for making their own clothes and other art projects."

Daisy glanced up from her drawing. "Cool clothes like Paisley's, or boring clothes like yours and Mum's?"

"Cool clothes like Paisley's," I guessed.

She put her pencil down. "I'm in."

~

The Swoosh Hutch was a former church, with attached church hall, in West Hobart, one of the inner city suburbs: nice front gardens, trendy coffee places on every corner, and street after street of restored weatherboard and red brick houses with unthinkably high rents. Trace, up and coming real estate agent that she is, gets very excited about how many old churches have come on the market in recent years. Most of them get converted into yoga studios or cafes, though a few make the full shift into private residences.

Living in a church does not appeal to me. Surely it would be draughty, and full of ghosts.

"So there are about forty general members," Paisley explained as I drove us there. "Members can use any of the equipment, reserve the space to run workshops, that sort of thing. I'm a general member, but I don't get in there often enough — mostly I drop by when I need to cut leather and denim. Their tool selection is dreamy. Oh, and sometimes I use the designing software to print my own fabric for a special project."

"Print your own fabric?" Daisy bounced. "Could I have a skirt with brains on it?"

"I mean, sure," said Paisley. "Obvs."

I could immediately think of some pretty cool uses for print-your-own fabric myself. Morgaine had hinted broadly I should pick up more sewing skills if I wanted to extend what I was doing at the shop, and I'd been trying to get up the courage. Maybe I should sign up as a member to this makerspace, get some practice in away from my employers so I could wow them with my new abilities. "It's just for garment making?"

"There are a couple of artists who specialise in other media — one who makes soft sculpture, a few jewellers. But all the equipment they've collected is based around fabricwork. That's why it's a makerspace, not a hacker-space — it's more specific. The only engineering we do involves cloth and thread."

"Forty general members. Does that mean there's another kind of member?"

"Sure, the studio members. The main makerspace is in the hall, but the old church itself is partitioned into four studios. The four original members of the board who crowdfunded the space to get it set up, they each got a studio. If one of them leaves, I think there's some sort of lottery for which of the general members gets the next spot? Studio members pay a higher membership fee, and they have a responsibility to help run the whole shebang."

"And one of those original members is Chameleon?"

"That's the rumour I heard."

"From a *very* reliable source?"

Paisley rolled their eyes at me. "If you want *very* reliable sources, let's call up Sergeant Torrance and see what he thinks?"

"No no, let's go with your friend-of-a-friend vague rumour."

We were going nowhere. This was probably a huge waste of time. But for some reason, I just couldn't let this drop. If nothing else, I wanted to find Chameleon so I could apologise for turning their first full fashion collection into my own Shakespearian costume party.

～

We had mistimed our visit… or perhaps, timed it perfectly. There was some kind of party going on as we stepped into the makerspace hall. The place was crowded with people, many of them clustered around a huge work table covered with garbage bags.

"Paisley!" A woman with bright, glossy white hair (dipped in purple at the ends) leaped out at us, giving Paisley a warm hug. "You made it! We don't usually see you at our Open Nights."

She was older than I'd expected — I assume by default that all of Paisley's friends are around twenty years old. This one was closer to my age, but infinitely cooler. Shifting from the super conservative wedding industry to the indie fashion world always made me feel just that bit more basic than everyone else, and this glamorous creature was the opposite of basic.

"Oops, Open Day, crowds everywhere, definitely not my thing," Paisley said faintly, giving me an apologetic look as they moved back out of the hug. "Hi, Meegan. This is Daisy and Sam. They were interested in seeing the place."

"All are welcome!" Meegan gave us the world's hugest grin, which showed off both of her piercings. Her white and purple hair was so glossy, it hurt the eyes. "Paisley, you have to join in the bin bag challenge, you are the reigning champion after last year. They made a dinner jacket out of a garbage bag," she added to me. "But there wasn't quite enough plastic to quilt the lapels and do full trousers… so Paisley did it with these tiny shorts under the jacket! Epic."

"What's the bin bag challenge?" piped up Daisy with

great interest.

"You get an hour to turn one standard plastic garbage bag into wearable fashion," said Paisley reluctantly. "I'm kind of brilliant at it."

"You are!" said Meegan. "Let's go, come on. You're just in time to sign up!"

"I'm helping you," said Daisy, crowding after Paisley. "I'm the best at scissors!"

Having lost my sidekicks, it was time for me to play lone fashion detective. I sidled through the crowd, collecting a jam jar mimosa for a $10 donation, pretending I was part of this arty, glam crowd.

I really was going to have to start making my own clothes.

The challenge began, in a hail of cheers. Scissors flew. Plastic ripped. I glanced over to check on Daisy and spotted her happily bossing Paisley around, waving a measuring tape as the two of them set to work.

Right, then.

I made my way through an ante-room used for storage, dodged around a pile of cardboard boxes, and opened doors until I found the right one leading into the main church. Jackpot!

My footsteps echoed on the polished boards as I stepped inside. Much like being around police officers, being in church always made me feel paranoid and slightly guilty. There's no tragic back story behind that one, it's just how I'm wired.

Still, I was practically on my tiptoes, creeping along like I had everything to hide. I wasn't supposed to be here.

Partition boards divided the huge space into four

decent-sized studios. The partitions went high enough you could stand in the space without making awkward eye contact over the top of them, which would be my first concern. Also, I suppose, artists need walls to hang things on.

The first studio, bearing a banner with the name Space Harpy, was full of glitter. Glitter was all I could see. Glitter fabric, glitter beads, glitter glitter. As anyone who regularly takes care of a primary school aged child knows, glitter is a dangerous ally. Working with it constantly required a certain amount of bravery.

Whoever Space Harpy was, they were clearly into making accessories. Glittery bags, shoes and tablet cases were scattered all over a work table, with finished pieces filed in cubby holes along one partition wall.

The next studio was more about what I think of as traditional fashion. Pencil sketches overlapping on the pin board, a fabric cutter, a few dresses on mannequins. This artist's drawing style didn't match with Chameleon's — the drawings I was looking at were more cartoony, less 'vintage Vogue'. But they were good. Many of the photos pinned to the back wall of finished projects were of theatre costumes, including a staging of *Cabaret* that I was sorry I'd missed out on seeing.

The third studio was empty. Just, completely empty. Stripped bare, all pin-pricked partition walls and polished floorboards. Interesting.

"Can I help you?"

I screamed and jumped, because I am an idiot. Still, I hadn't been expecting a voice right there, behind me. I spun around and saw a young man, skinny in drainpipe jeans and a Placebo t-shirt. His blue hair was spiky, he had about five piercings in one ear, and he was smirking at me like I was the funniest thing he'd seen all day.

"I'm sorry," I gasped. "I didn't think anyone was in here."

"Clearly," he said, rolling his eyes. "Having a nose about, were you, or just trying to escape the dressmaking disco out there?"

A loud, raucous wave of delight echoed through the old church from the garbage bag party going on next door.

"Both," I admitted.

"Don't blame you. I get why Harper and Meegan like to stage these little fundraisers. We rely on all the membership fees people sink into this place but never follow through on."

"Like a gym, then." Good business model, if you can get it. Profit off people's good intentions and inherent laziness.

He snapped his fingers and smiled. "Exactly like a gym. Coffee?"

I had finished my mimosa, which meant I was holding an empty jam jar like an idiot. "Yes please. I'm Sam."

"Leon." He took the jam jar off me and led me into his corner of the studio space, the only one I hadn't yet investigated. He rinsed my jar in a long sink that ran against the outer wall. It must have been plumbed in specially, as I couldn't think of any reason there would be a sink like that in the original church design.

"I have the sink and most of the electrical sockets in my corner, which means I get to provide all the cuppas," said Leon, lifting a mug off a shelf for himself. "I can do you strong black tea, or cheap instant coffee. No milk or sugar, because I'm lazy and I don't shop."

"Coffee, please. Did you put the sink in yourself?"

"Me, no!" Leon barked with laughter. "My plumbing skills are basically... well, I can sew. This was a stretch goal — you know we crowdfunded the space?"

"I'd heard."

"We have a long lease with a chill landlord who said it was fine to put the sink in as long as we paid a professional to install it. So we told our backers if we just raised five thousand dollars over our goal, Leon would have his painting sink! And here we are."

"Nice. We have four bathtubs at the shop where I work — for all the dyeing."

"Brilliant!" said Leon, recognising me as a fellow artist. "I have to go outside if I want to dye anything. The others are worried I'd make too much of a mess of the floorboards. Like Harper's glitter is ever coming out."

I glanced around at his work. He was tidier than the other two, but I could see shelves and shelves of folded jeans, plus a photo wall showing various denim garments that had been hacked, slashed, painted, distressed and patterned with bleach. Another upcycler! And not a swatch of white satin in sight.

He clearly liked to paint denim: the jeans he was currently wearing had adorable black bats painted all over them. In one of his pics, he modelled a jacket with a giant cartoon frog on the back.

The only example of women's fashion I saw on his photo wall was a ballgown made out of what looked like a bunch of pockets cut off several hundred pairs of old jeans.

I instantly coveted it, even though I'd never have anywhere to wear it, not in a decade of Saturday nights.

The jug whistled, and Leon took it off the boil to make our cheap instant coffees while I tried to think of a way to drop Chameleon into the conversation. Should I just tell my funny story about dyeing ten designer wedding dresses bright green? It was one hell of an ice breaker.

It occurred to me that this was, in fact, going to be my go-to ice breaker story for the rest of my life.

"That bitch!" A girl in silver cargo pants and a bright white t-shirt, her black hair caught up in a silver scrunchie, whirled into Leon's studio and hopped up on to the table, sitting on a pile of painted denims. "I can't believe she's trying to replace E.J. already!"

I smiled awkwardly.

The girl, who had so much glitter lip gloss on that I could only assume this was Space Harpy, stared at me. "Who are you?"

"This is Sam, she's stickybeaking," said Leon, handing me my jam jar back, full of instant coffee and wrapped in a paint-flecked paper napkin so I didn't burn my fingers. "This is Harper Park, she's rude."

Since I was officially stickybeaking, I guess I could ask nosy questions. Score! "Who's E.J.?" I asked, and sipped my horrifically hot coffee.

"The empty studio," said Leon, in a fake-spooky voice as if he was trying to be ironic about it. He turned away quickly, though, looking genuinely upset. "E.J. died recently. It sucks. Meegan's pushing to get a new studio member in straight away. The rest of us want to take more than five minutes to get over it."

"Bad enough she packed up all his gear so quickly," Harper growled, her hands flexing like she wanted to claw out a throat with her acrylics. "Not like his horrible family even bothered to collect it. But seriously, she's out there teasing a bunch of our regulars that we'll be holding the lottery soon, when we *agreed* to wait at least a month out of respect. And when I said that to her face, she was so patronising about how much we need the money coming in. Seriously. She treats me like a kid."

"What sort of clothes did E.J. design?" I asked, keeping my questions light and only mildly nosy.

Both their faces closed over.

"Pyjamas," said Leon, colder than before. "Hadn't you get back to the party?"

It's important to know when to make a swift exit, and I had left my nine-year-old niece in a busy hall surrounded by strangers and scissors. "Nice to meet you," I said, toasting Leon lightly with my jam jar full of coffee. I took it with as I withdrew.

They both started talking quietly together almost as soon as I left, but I was already feeling guilty about my levels of stickybeaking, and didn't linger to eavesdrop.

I did take a closer look at the boxes stacked up in the storeroom on my way back to the Great Bin Bag Challenge, which was noisy with screams and shouts like they were in the middle of a horse race.

The boxes all had the name E.J. written on them in sharpie. Most of them were taped up, but I spotted one that looked like it had an open flap.

Before I could tell myself not to, I opened the box.

8

"BOTTLE TOPS?" REPEATED TRACE, AS WE SHARED A LATE night ice cream raid. Daisy was in bed, clutching her 3rd prize trophy from the Swoosh Hutch contest (a squeaky rubber octopus with a 3 painted on its head). She had to be cajoled deeply to sleep in her pyjamas and not the surprisingly natty 'goth doctor's coat' she and Paisley had constructed out of crackling black plastic.

"Bottle tops," I confirmed. "A whole box of them in different colours! From soft drink bottles. So I guess whoever E.J. is, he was very much into art from recycled materials."

"But you definitely think E.J. is Ethan Brady."

"It's a hell of a coincidence if he's not. I mean, Hobart can't have produced that many tragic fashion-connected deaths in the last few weeks. And his name starts with E."

"Did you look up Ethan Brady's middle name?"

"David."

"That doesn't start with a J."

"No, it does not." I shrugged, taking one more

spoonful of boysenberry ripple. "And his Dad's name is Gavin so it's not going to be Ethan Jr. I still can't quite wrap my head around the idea of a gym-obsessed car salesman in his mid-thirties who was a secret fashion designer. Even if he did have a covert design studio, that doesn't mean he was actually Chameleon. But it might explain the roomful of random wedding dresses in his house."

"Does it, though?" Trace said in a deadpan voice. "Does it really explain anything?"

"No," I moaned. "It does not explain anything."

"I still don't get why you're still poking into this…" Her face turned impish. "Unless this is an excuse to text your high school crush."

"He was not my crush. And I definitely am not going to text Donovan."

"Not even to tell him that there may be a bunch of boxes of his brother's things that no one has bothered to collect?"

"I'm not texting him because I do not have his number."

"Oh," said Trace.

"Yeah."

"Sam, I'm starting to think that you are in fact, not a fashion detective after all. At least, not a very good one."

"I know," I said glumly. "Me too."

Part of me was sort of hoping that Donovan Brady would arrive on my doorstep again the next morning, coffee cups in both hands, begging me to help him with his wedding dress investigation.

That way, I'd be able to casually drop the fashion designer brother theory on him, and judge his reaction while sipping a delicious vanilla latte. Also, I could collect his phone number in case any other brilliant bits of evidence wafted in my general direction while I was totally not investigating anything.

Unfortunately, he never showed up.

"Chameleon was at the Swoosh Hutch last night," Paisley hissed at me when I entered Fashionably Late. (Completely on time, ha, like we don't make that joke eight times a week.)

I blinked rapidly at them. "What are you talking about?"

Paisley pushed their phone at me, open to Instagram. "See?"

It was indeed a photo of the winner of the contest, posted from Chameleon's account. A space age black mini and crop top. Nicely shaped, but generic. The photo framed the winner's trophy (a rubber shark, not as cool than Daisy's octopus) and left out the head of the winner altogether. It did have a #swooshhutch hashtag, though, so wasn't trying to be all that subtle. "You were robbed," I said, pushing Paisley's phone back, thinking hard. If Ethan Brady was Chameleon, and Ethan Brady was dead, who was posting from Chameleon's account? "Your doctor's coat was way more original."

"Eh, Daisy and I had fun. She was inspired, and I was happy to assist. Too much to hope she'll go into the rag trade?"

"Meegan was certainly encouraging her! She showed Daisy the fabric printer before we left," I added in explanation to Morgaine, who was sitting peacefully at the counter with her cup of rooibos, ignoring us both. "Daisy woke me and Trace up at six this morning, begging to go back to the Swoosh Hutch so she can make bedsheets with her favourite illustrations from the Encyclopaedia of Anatomy."

"Did you explain to her about copyright?" asked Paisley

"She assured me she could recreate the drawings in crayon."

"Should be all right, then."

"Sam," Morgaine interrupted. "Sorry to ask with such late notice, but can you work tomorrow? And stay late tonight?"

I didn't usually come in on Saturdays unless Morgaine was going to be away for the weekend. Staying late into Friday night was unheard of. But it wasn't like I had anything else to do. "Sure, what's up?"

"I'll need your help with some dyeing tonight, and the photo shoot tomorrow."

"No worries." Wait. "What photo shoot?"

"Oh," said Paisley, putting their phone back in their pocket. "That was the other news. Wait until you hear!"

~

Addie Chambers, the woman in linens who had barged into the shop the other day asking questions about wedding dresses, turned out to be *Impeccable Magazine*'s art director. She was also a champion problem-solver. She and Morgaine had figured out a solution to the Chameleon bridal shoot, and... it was a pretty great one.

You might ask, how is it possible to do a full wedding-themed magazine shoot without wedding dresses? I'd love to be mysterious and say 'they did it with mirrors' but the truth is? They used the green ones.

They also clawed back all five of the still-white gowns thanks to some hefty negotiation — according to Morgaine, Donovan paid off the brides in full *and* promised they could have the dresses back after the shoot — plus they'd be able to tell everyone they were married wearing Chameleon originals instead of the original label-less situation. The brides all had wedding dates more than two months away, which meant their dresses would appear in the magazine first... and they were each guaranteed to be the only bride wearing that unique gown. Funnily enough, they all leaped at that deal.

Addie and her team brought in heaps of trailing ivy and other leafy fronds, real plants as well as green and purple silk flowers. The models wearing white gowns were draped in green leafiness... and the green brides were given long, flowing green veils and floral tiaras, making them look like something out of, well. Fairyland.

The loss for this season's teen shoppers for formal frocks would be high fashion's gain.

I personally had been up half the night dyeing the veils to match the gowns. Luckily tulle didn't take long to dry! I still hadn't emptied one of the dye baths in case we had to nip back in a hurry and turn something else green.

(Not wanting to waste it, I'd dyed a few of my own things at the same time. A favourite old faded cream shirt, and one of Aunt Harriet's lace cushions which was discoloured after a Daisy+Peanut Butter incident. Why yes, I was becoming one of those people who looks at a damaged item and thinks: "I can fix it with my skills!")

"One green wedding dress is a mistake, but ten green wedding dresses? That's a statement," announced Addie Chambers, pleased with herself. "We've been doing all-white shoots for decades, and our readers must be sick of the whole champagne vs white gold vs ecru debate. Time to change the narrative."

"She's quoting me," said Morgaine in an undertone.

"I hope they're giving the shop credit," I hissed back at her.

"Oh, yes! This will be the Chameleon Collection, styled by Fashionably Late."

"What if the real designer comes out of the woodwork and complains about what we're doing?"

"Addie seemed confident that she had the contract lawyers on her side."

I bet she did.

Besides, I was pretty sure that Chameleon was dead.

Addie had ditched the original rural farmyard idea (so much for all of Donovan's hectic negotiations about haybales) and found a new, equally rustic location on the same farming property in Grove, not far from Huonville. This was a gorgeous vale, with lush green foliage and a gently babbling brook. The models all went barefoot, which was an interesting choice considering the number of snakes, spiders and rogue blackberry bushes you might expect in any Tasmanian backyard, yet alone the country. Still, they all looked like adorable woodland nymphs, and no one requested any bandaids, so it probably turned out fine.

The brides who were so generous to lend us the dresses might find them returned with a few mud streaks. Spring in Tasmania generally means everything gets soggy around the edges.Those of us not being photographed had all brought gumboots and did not regret that life choice.

And that was before the miniature goats came to the party: three of them, watchfully guarded by a couple of rugged men in flannel, trotting across the film set and bleating lovingly at the fake brides in their fairy bower.

"You did really well with those colours," Morgaine said quietly to me, at one point. "You're getting more confident with dye, I like it."

I was warmed by the compliment. "Are we returning to Diana's classic No Weddings policy in future?"

"Sure," Morgaine said. "Except for the part where we're appearing in a national bridal magazine as a stylist for wedding dresses. I'm sure that will have no effect on our future business decisions at all."

Diana didn't turn up to the shoot herself, saying "I did all that in the 70s, darling."

I didn't get a chance to talk to Donovan all day. He was busy wearing sunglasses at people, making sure the access road didn't fill up with casual onlookers. The collection was still supposed to be mostly secret.

I was on veil patrol: supplying, tidying, mending and on one memorable occasion, ripping to shreds (because a tiny hole in a veil is anathema, but deliberate rips apparently look like high art).

Nothing of any note happened, apart from a warming sense of professional pride, though at one point one of the attractive flannel-clad goat farmers found himself surrounded by staring, thoughtful, jaded magazine people.

"What are they looking at?" he asked me out of the corner of his mouth, sidling away from Addie Chambers and her assistants. Clearly I was the most normal person in the vicinity. Everyone else was gazing at him like he was the second coming of Hugh Jackman.

"You've heard of being mentally undressed?" I told him, helpfully. "Well, they're mentally *dressing* you in designer gear. I'd say you're about five minutes away from being dragged into the photo shoot."

"Oh, no." The farmer seized the nearest miniature goat and hefted it carefully against his chest. "That's not happening. Bry!" he yelled to his brother. "Back to work!"

The other goat farmer nodded, rounded up the remaining miniature goats, and the two of them disappeared faster than you can say 'naturally distressed flannel.'

The second location was even more impressive, because Addie Chambers managed to talk someone into roping off a huge section of Kingston Beach so she could get shots of two brides walking hand in hand through the gentle late afternoon surf.

I couldn't imagine how much red tape they'd had to slash and burn to make this happen, on a weekend where the beach was usually packed. Especially since this all came about after her first visit to Morgaine at the shop, only a couple of days previously.

Some people were born to get things done.

Donovan's job was a lot more complicated here. He had team of about six men and women, all in intimidating suit jackets over black t-shirts (with the words Brick Wall prominently displayed), spread out across the walkway above the beach. They had the assistance of the local police, too — an official taped barrier and several officers on the ground. I was keeping my distance.

The road in front of Fashionably Late and the other shops was blocked off, to try to keep the crowds away from the beach, but what happened was that everyone parked around the corner, and arrived on foot. Without all the usual cars in the way, there was extra room for sticky beakers to cluster along the strip and watch the action.

Not that there was a lot of action, but hey. The dresses were pretty.

Since no customers could get to us, Paisley closed the shop and came to watch as the brides walked barefoot on the sand, posed on rocks, and looked conventionally attractive.

I had no official role now, as the veils were a) white and b) fine. Addie had chosen white dresses for this more public shoot, holding back the pixie green as a surprise so it didn't get raked over social media before anyone saw it in the magazine.

I got the impression that this part of the shoot *was* designed to get leaked on social media, since the security team made no effort to stop the many, many phones pointed at the bridal models.

I saw a flash of white and purple hair in the crowd and recognised Meegan from the Swoosh Hutch, standing with Leon and Harper. All three of them looked sombre and thoughtful. Which... really did support my theory about Ethan being Chameleon. If anyone had witnessed him working on those dresses, designing or making them, it would have been these three.

I glanced around to see if Paisley was nearby to be sent over for some covert spy work, but I couldn't see them.

A big black SUV pulled up against the barrier and parked illegally. I saw Donovan jog lightly in that direction to tell them to move... but before he could, the driver got out and started yelling at him. It was Jeena Harding-Brady. She wore another killer short dress, this one in blinding white instead of the black she'd worn for her husband's funeral. Her makeup and blonde ponytail were on point.

She looked furious.

Donovan reached his sister-in-law, obviously trying to get her to quiet down, but it didn't work. The two of them had a short, but heated argument. Jeena looked like she was about ready to throttle him, but finally she hopped back into her giant car, backed up and drove away.

It must have annoyed her how silent the electric car was. No growly engine to express her rage.

I intercepted him as he headed back towards the crowd. "What was that about?"

Donovan shook his head impatiently. "More Jeena drama. She said the whole point of selling the dresses was to make them disappear, and this is the opposite of that. She's really not your biggest fan right now, by the way."

"I'm heart-broken." And really hoping she didn't sue me. Surely the NDA I signed was no longer relevant, given that the dresses had not even been owned by her when she 'sold' them to us. "Did she say anything about your brother?"

"Why would she?"

This was bound to be the part where I ended up looking like an idiot. "I was wondering if it ever crossed your mind that Ethan might have designed the dresses himself?"

Donovan stared blankly. "Ethan. My brother Ethan?"

I explained briefly what I'd found out at the Swoosh Hutch. "Was he artistic at all? Did he draw or make things as a hobby?"

"I mean, he wanted to design CD covers when he was a teenager, but our dad squashed that hard. Dad has a — pretty narrow view of how men are supposed to behave."

I looked at him sideways. "How does he feel about you working for a fashion magazine?"

"I emphasise the 'security' and 'owns my own busi-ness' side," Donovan said darkly. "Anyway, I have plenty of non-fashion clients. I shouldn't have to cover up what I do, but I'm only down here a couple of times a year, why give him an excuse to do his nut? Not that anything short of selling cars for his business will ever be good enough anyway." He scanned the crowd. Did you say they were here? These Swoosh kids?"

"Not kids," I said, pulling him closer to the edge of the beach for a line of sight. "There, see? The guy with sunflowers painted on his jeans, next to that woman with the sparkles on her face. The other one, with the white and purple hair, that's Meegan."

Of the three of them, watching the photo shoot, Meegan looked the most troubled, and the most artistic. She wore a fluttery over-sized shirt over a sleeveless green tee, and a purple denim skirt that matched the stripe on her hair.

"Meegan?" Donovan repeated. "You didn't say her name was Meegan."

"Didn't I?"

Ignoring me, he strode off, using all his intimidating suit powers to part the crowd. Well, fine.

I still didn't have his number. Good thing I was not going to be discovering any more clues on his behalf. No reason to text him, no reason to be remotely interested in what he was up to.

"Sam!"

Paisley popped up behind me, windswept and panicked. "They need you down on the sand. Addie called you her veil stylist, or something? There's a tulle emergency."

I sighed. "I'm coming, I'm coming."

Weddings. Why did my life always circle back to weddings?

9

FINALLY THE SHOOT WOUND DOWN, THE ROAD WAS OPENED up, and the onlookers wandered away. Addie Chambers bundled her models into a giant rental trailer that they were using for combined frock storage and change room. The photographers and security team drifted towards the pub, job done.

Morgaine headed home in search of a long bath and a deep glass of wine, or possibly the other way around. Paisley bopped off in the other direction, probably to spend Saturday night going to six different parties, drinking things I've never heard of, and recording it all on Instagram.

I bundled up the stray veils, intending to drop them back at the shop since no one else seemed interested in preserving them. Before I could head back over the road, though, Donovan appeared again, swinging around the side of the trailer all of a sudden. "Samantha," he said, as if I was the one who had startled him.

I raised my armful of tulle and voile. "All's well that ends well, eh?"

"Addie seems happy," he said in the sort of voice you reserve for people who are never, ever happy. "That should keep the magazine from asking too many awkward questions about how my security team lost fifteen wedding dresses."

Hmm, that sentence didn't sound quite as final as it should. "But?"

"But we still haven't located the Titania. And a certain high maintenance pop star will be arriving at Hobart airport in two days, expecting to be introduced to her epic wedding dress."

His voice was grim, but his eyes were sad. Damn it, why do I find that appealing in a man? This is how my husband suckered me in when I was twenty-two and so much softer than I am now. Now, at least, I'm old enough and cynical enough to recognise it happening, and stop myself from making mistakes quite as terrible as I made in my past. Like trying to fulfil the emotional needs of pretty men. I patted his arm with mild sympathy. "This sounds like a you problem."

His mouth twitched. "Really, you're not at all curious?"

"Done with curiosity, done with fashion detective work!" I informed him cheerfully. "It's the weekend. I'm off the clock."

Donovan quickly changed the subject, or so I thought. "I saw Meegan earlier, with her friends. I showed her a picture, and you were right about her E.J. being my brother. I called my father to see if anyone had been in touch about some boxes of Ethan's to collect and he went quiet. Didn't bother with Jeena, because she's still pitching a fit over these wedding dresses."

"Little did we realise when she sold us the dresses, she was hoping we would destroy them," I said solemnly. "I wish I'd known. I've always wanted to experiment with tie-dye."

"Anyway. I'm heading over to the Swoosh Hutch later to check out the boxes and see for myself. Want to tag along?"

I shouldn't be tempted. It was my day off, and I'd spent most of it working. Why on earth would I follow a man who didn't even remember me from high school, to collect boxes belonging to his dead brother, in the hopes of solving the mystery of that dead brother's secret double life as a fashion designer?

More to the point, why did Donovan even want me to come?

And that question, more than any other, was why I rolled my eyes and said "Fine. But you're buying dinner afterwards."

I used to live on a constant tightrope of stress, spreadsheets, management tactics. Planning other people's weddings meant I was constantly solving problems, challenging myself, facing down bushfires of chaos with my own skills of calmness and reason. I always had a backup venue, if the dream location fell through. I always had a contingency plan if there was a catering disaster, a wardrobe malfunction, or an unexpected ex causing trouble. I always had a box of tissues within arm's reach. And I loved how damned good I was at my job.

Then it all came crashing down. My husband vanished to Bali with not only our savings, but hundreds of thousands of dollars of other people's money. Twelve weddings were ruined, and at least two of the couples broke up during the chaos that followed. My beloved business, built up from nothing, was suddenly poison in an industry that's all about goodwill and word of mouth. Our assets — including my car, and the house I'd poured so much time and money and care into — were frozen and later had to be sold to cover legal fees.

It was the worst year of my life. I lost everything... and for a while there it looked like I might end up in prison myself.

It worked out okay, in the end. My sister, who had her own drama to deal with, shared her aunt-in-law's home with me — a literal soft place to fall. Diana Wave offered me a job. Finally, I found a calmness in not being constantly on the edge.

Things were good now. No one was trying to ruin me. I hardly even got hate mail any more, as long as I stayed away from most forms of social media, and any public event featuring someone who knew one of the families affected by my husband's crime. (So, most of Hobart, small cities are the worst.)

I don't miss him. I don't even miss the business, not really. It's hard to be nostalgic for all the good stuff when the bad is so very recent. But I miss the person I used to be, before the revelations and the betrayal and my actual, literal arrest. Samantha Sullivan, champion problem-solver. Fixer of disasters. Smoother of hiccups.

When I looked into Donovan Brady's big sad eyes, I

wanted to solve all his problems. I recognised this impulse in myself. It wasn't healthy, and it wouldn't end well.

But... maybe I could risk one more outing as a fashion detective, before I hung up my heels and went back to being a plain old stress-free shop girl.

What harm could it do?

The Swoosh Hutch was closed and locked up, which did not improve Donovan's mood. He was quiet and twitchy for the whole drive, which I suppose was fair enough. He'd just learned a massive new thing about Ethan, and it was clearly doing his head in.

Still, that didn't make it any less awkward to be hovering around a closed church hall, looking for a way in.

"Maybe they got delayed coming back from the beach?" I suggested. It was late Saturday evening, after all. Surely the bright young things had better things to do than hang out at work, even if they were dedicated to their art.

Donovan frowned. "Meegan said they were coming back straight away. I was hoping to talk to her again about my brother."

"They're artists, maybe they were distracted by a passing butterfly." I was rapidly regretting my impulse to support Donovan in his time of stress. He had a look in his eye that made me suspect I was about five minutes away from being implicated in a break and enter. "Did you get her number? You said you knew her."

"I knew of her," he corrected. "Jeena was convinced that Ethan was messing around on her. She'd mentioned a

Meegan once or twice. Ethan said she was a friend." He waved a frustrated hand. "Obviously he was being secretive, but no one had any idea the friendship involved secret fashion design."

I guess all families think theirs is normal. "Why would he keep this whole *Impeccable* deal from Jeena? Especially if she thought he was cheating on her. From your dad, okay, that makes sense. But his wife?"

Donovan looked thoughtful. "So you do think he and Meegan were together?"

I'm not saying I have a tendency to think the worst of married men these days, but my husband did take our personal assistant with him to Bali along with all the money he stole. So yeah. Assuming the best is not my brand any more.

"I think anyone who is capable of hiding a time consuming hobby and/or second job from his wife is probably also capable of cheating on her," I said. "Or for some reason thought it was fine to let her think he was cheating on her, to cover up a second job, which… well, that's also betrayal."

Donovan leaned into the door of the church hall again, knocking loudly. "You think keeping secrets about money is worse than sex with someone else?"

"Betrayal is betrayal," I said, managing to keep my voice steady. "Financial secrets hurt too. How much did you say *Impeccable* paid Chameleon?"

"We don't know for sure that Ethan is…" he started.

"Sure. Maybe it was Meegan and he acted as the agent." No reason to mention that I'd seen Meegan's art style and it didn't match. That wasn't enough to go on until I got my hands on some examples of Ethan's own art style. "Maybe Chameleon is really some twelve-year-old kid in China and Ethan was playing middle man. How much money are we talking about?"

Donovan winced. "Ten grand for the exclusive photo rights to use the collection for the magazine. Fifty for the Titania commission."

"Fifty thousand dollars?" My voice went a bit shrill.

"She's a pop star. Her wedding is a big deal. Which, incidentally, is why finding the dress is a priority. Insurance is all very well, but Ethan's estate may end up liable for all that money — including the *Impeccable* photo rights — if we can't find, photograph and deliver the Titania to Colette Cray."

"Sixty thousand dollars is a lot of spare cash to hide from your wife," I remarked.

Donovan's face went very flat. "Yes. Yes, it is."

I was no longer wondering why Jeena looked so furious on the day of her husband's funeral, and again earlier today. This was clearly about more than a room full of wedding dresses.

A beaten-up old car covered in Pride stickers pulled up into the tiny church carpark, and Leon climbed out in those sunflower jeans of his. He was on his own, hauling a giant sack of what I assumed was more denim to reclaim. (I had to wonder if they had a proper laundry set up like ours, or if they had to use home machines or one of the last surviving Laundromats in the city.)

"You can't get enough of the place," Leon said cheerfully, addressing me as he approached. His eyes darted the bulky form of Donovan with a certain degree of apprehension, but his tone stayed light. "Thinking of signing that talented niece of yours up for a membership?"

"This is Donovan Brady," I blurted out. "He's E.J.'s brother."

Leon slowed his walk, eyeing Donovan more openly. "Yup. I see the resemblance. Shoulders."

"I spoke to Meegan about collecting his things." Donovan reached into his wallet, but Leon waved him away as he unlocked the side door.

"Normally I'd ask for ID, don't get me wrong. But I recognise the car." Leon gave us a kind of sickly smile as he pointed back at the big green SUV. Licence plate: GAV-002. I hadn't quite put it together that Donovan was driving his brother's car, but it would of course be the most easily available loaner for his family to provide.

Was it weird that they all drove matching cars with their dad's name on the license plate? I was pretty sure that wasn't a normal family thing.

The Swoosh Hutch had a different vibe this time, with no arty party atmosphere. The wooden floorboards creaked underfoot, and the tables and floor had all been swept clean.

"Don't talk to me about Meegan," Leon grumbled as he switched on a few lights and led them through to the storage room. "Stroppy cow went and disappeared on us at the beach. Harper and I spent ages hunting for her. Turns out she hitched a lift to a friend's place and was halfway through a bottle of cheap red when she finally got around to texting, thanks *so much* for taking ten years off my life." He dragged a hand through his spiky hair.

"Probably for the best," said Donovan. "My sister-in-law is on the warpath. Meegan might not want to be found."

Leon blinked several times. "E.J. was married? That is… new information."

"He and Meegan were an item, then," I remarked casually, not even making it a question. You get the best gossip by pretending you've heard it already.

Leon hummed. "I couldn't *possibly* comment."

Instead of taking the boxes out to his SUV straight away, Donovan dragged a few of them out on to the floor and started going through them. He went for the untaped one first, the one I already knew was full of plastic bottle tops.

Leon, apparently not bothered about us taking up his time, hopped up on a nearby table and watched with interest. Surely he already knew the contents, if he was there when Meegan boxed everything up. In which case, we were the show he was interested in.

Donovan scooped half-heartedly through the bottle tops, to check there was nothing else under them, and then ripped the tape off another box. He glanced up at me. "Want to help?"

We both knew curiosity was a big part of why I was here. I had convinced myself that I wanted to be helpful, but why pretend I wasn't also super nosy? I lifted down a few boxes of my own to rifle through.

"What are you looking for?" Leon asked.

"Among other things," said Donovan. "Colette Cray's missing wedding dress."

"Fuuuu…. Far out," said Leon. "Actual Colette Cray?

The pop star? Not some random old lady with the same name?"

The boxes contained exactly the sort of things you might find when packing up a whole fashion studio. Fabrics, good stuff, folded neatly into sealed plastic bags. Haberdashery tools, magazines.

I found a box full of satin and lace scraps in different shades of white, nothing that exactly matched the wedding dresses but... it was the first real indication of a connection. I showed a handful of the white fabric to Donovan.

"If you need me to make this green, just say the word."

He sputtered something that was almost a laugh.

My next box was another winner: salvaged chip and lolly packets, sorted by colour.

"E.J. was big on recycled materials," said Leon dryly. "Ethical fashion can save the planet if you charge enough for it..."

Donovan sat back on his heels and shook his head. "None of this feels like him. I can't picture it. How long was he even working here?"

Leon shrugged one skinny shoulder. "Five years or so? It was just me and Meegan at first, running the whole thing on the sniff of an oily rag. We met Harper when we did a reclaimed fashion workshop up at Elizabeth College — she started coming around after that, and brought a bunch of her tiny student friends. They were all willing to kick in a chunk of their pocket money to use our machines, and that kept the lights on. We were still only using the hall at that point, paying month to month. Not the church itself. Then one day I walked in and E.J. was sitting out there with Meegan, in one of those gorgeous suits of his, talking about business models and crowdfunding."

"So he provided business advice." Clearly that made more sense to Donovan than his brother playing with satins and thread.

"Sure, that's what he said at first, but after a few drinks it all came out — he'd wanted to work in fashion for ages, repressive macho dad wouldn't let him take the courses he wanted, forced him into the family business, whatever. Poor little rich boy. E.J. had stacks and stacks of ideas and sketches, but couldn't sew a straight line to save his life. So we turned him into a… project, I suppose. Taught him everything. All very *My Fair Lady*, only the end result was Richard Gere making Julia Roberts do all his homework for him."

I gave him an odd look. "Are we still talking about *My Fair Lady*?"

"It's possible I'm thinking of *Pretty Woman*," admitted Leon. "But with pocket squares. Either way, I didn't get to kiss the boy. This was Meegan's romantic comedy, all the way."

The next box I opened was piled high with sketch-books, some of them looking kind of faded and dusty. I pulled one out and flipped through: it was filled with fashion drawings. The sketches were formal in style, and while these weren't as good as the bridal examples I'd seen Donovan flashing around from the recent collection, they were a lot closer to Chameleon's drawings than anything else I had seen around here.

The first book was frocks, mostly — cute but basic with a few twirls here and there. They got more complex as the book went on. Another book was full of male clothes designs, all tailored shirts and bold patterns.

"Ethan was interested in menswear?" I said in surprise.

"Sure. E.J. didn't really have the skills to make that stuff — proper tailoring is the boss level of fashion work. So he worked on women's clothes at first, but his heart wasn't in it. He always said if he could save enough money he'd go off train properly under a real tailor, take a few years in Melbourne or Paris or whatever. We all knew he wasn't going anywhere. Not willing to risk being cut off from Daddy's money." Leon sounded kind of bitter about that.

I pulled out another sketchbook. This one was more current — floaty, flowy gowns that weren't quite the recent Chameleon collection, but felt like they'd poured from the same pencil. They were covered in notes, scribbled pointing out all the flaws in the designs. *Too narrow. Needs a flare. Make this better. Wrong colour. What were you thinking?*

"He was his own worst critic, apparently," said Leon lightly. "You wouldn't know it to talk to him. Ego the size of the Derwent River."

"So," I said. "You crowdfunded the makerspace and the studios, to expand what you were doing. What, three years ago?"

"About that."

"Did E.J. help?"

"I mean, he didn't work his butt off on Insta like Harper and Meegan. And he wouldn't tell any of his rich friends who we were or what we were doing, because he didn't want his family to find out. But I'm pretty sure he sunk extra funds in when we weren't looking. There were a couple of anonymous donations we didn't look at too closely. He and Meegs worked a lot on the t-shirt designs we used as rewards," Leon added, grudgingly.

Donovan pulled a shimmering length of red fabric out of another box. It reminded me a lot of a certain celebrity suit that had made Chameleon's reputation soar. The crime awards dress.

"So," I said, glancing over at Leon. "How long have you all known E.J. was Chameleon?"

Leon's face went very still. "What?"

"You know. Big successful up and coming totally secret fashion designer. The one behind all those bridal gowns they were showing off on the beach today, that the three of you specifically came to observe. There's no way he could have done all that — frocks for celebrities, magazine deals, a fifteen gown collection…"

"Sixteen," Donovan coughed.

"Without help. Without the three people he shared studio space with knowing exactly what he was doing. So did you help him cover it up, or were you actually involved in making the collection? Is that why you were so keen to see the photo shoot?"

Leon was outright staring at us now, like we were crazy. "What are you talking about?" he said finally. "E.J. was not Chameleon. He couldn't sew that well."

"Then who —" Donovan started, then broke off as we heard someone yelling outside the hall.

I thought it was some drunk at first, then realised that whoever it was — a male, deep, angry voice — they were bellowing Donovan's name.

"Friend of yours?" Leon asked in an acid tone.

Donovan took a deep breath and stood up, his arms full of shining red satin. "That's my dad," he said, like he was bracing himself for the worst. "He must have tracked my car. Stay here. I'll handle this."

10

I HADN'T EXACTLY MET GAVIN BRADY BEFORE, UNLESS
you counted my brief glimpse of him at Jeena and Ethan's
house earlier in the week. I knew of him, though. Not from
school — it was high school, we barely saw glimpses of
each other's parents, and didn't care enough to pay attention unless they were attached to our closest friends.

But this was Gavin Brady, the guy who took credit for
'turning Tasmania electric.' He and his car yard had
contributed massively to the rising popularity in fully electric vehicles over the last few years, something that had
been a hard sell across Australia generally.

This is a country where masculinity has snorted diesel
fumes ever since engines were invented.

Gavin Brady, with his cheesy homemade TV ads and
his big, booming voice, made the startling decision about
half a decade ago to turn his car yard (really four car yards,
across the state) fully electric. He didn't sell little
runaround cars, either — or if he did, they were hidden
behind the giant SUVs, massive boofy-looking monster

trucks that could take on a dirt road, a dodgy highway and a sudden wombat collision, all without breaking a sweat.

In a world that was increasingly gender-fluid, Gavin Brady was an old school dinosaur with one bright idea: he sold the male power fantasy while saving the world. Which... I mean, it worked. Wealthy Tasmanians took up electric vehicles in droves, which had the effect of bringing the price down across the board, making it slightly more affordable for the less-wealthy of us. As far as the average person on the street was concerned, good old Gaz was a dead-set legend.

One of these days I might be shocked to learn about a hugely successful businessman who is all smiles in public but turns out to be a horrendous arsehole behind closed doors. Today was not that day.

Leon and I hung back under the covered porch in front of the church hall, staying out of view of the two men fighting in the car park. Donovan and his father Gavin were similar heights, similar builds, and it was scary to see how angry they were at each other. They yelled and gestured with aggressive, barely-restrained power — sooner or later, one of them was going to throw a punch, and it wouldn't be pretty.

Donovan worked security, I remembered all over again. Right now, facing off against the unsettling barely-restrained violence of his father arguing, I could well believe he was capable of restraining someone hard.

"E.J. used to get that way sometimes," Leon said in a low voice. "So angry you thought he might — I don't know, punch his way through a wall or something. He and Meegan got into a fight once, about one of those secret late night shared projects that his wife probably doesn't know about. He stood over her, shouting like he couldn't stop. She turned around, stabbed his latest shirt design with a pair of scissors and left. Didn't see her around here for a week, not until he apologised."

"Like father, like son," I murmured.

"Yeah," said Leon, withdrawing even further up against the door. "When I heard Ethan died in a hit-and-run, first thing I thought was that he must have yelled at the wrong person."

It was surreal and kind of scary, watching Donovan lose his cool like this. It made me realise how little I really knew about him. We'd had like three conversations at high school beyond saying 'hey' when you pass someone in the corridor. Two of them had been about homework. One was a lingering conversation in a library containing some of my best flirtatious banter of all time, which is a weird thing to peak at when you're sixteen.

He didn't remember me.

We weren't friends. I was his weird fashion detective sidekick or something. I was convenient. An emotional support person with a weirdly specific knowledge base.

As I peeked around the corner, Donovan gave his dad one last angry shove, stormed to his (his brother's) green car and got into the passenger seat, handing over the keys. His father, still fuming, climbed into the driver's seat, then backed out of the car park.

"Wait," I said slowly.

"Wasn't he your ride?" asked Leon.

"Yes. He bloody was!"

My mouth fell open as Donovan and his dad both

drove away in that enormous silent car, neither of them giving a glance in the direction of me or the church hall.

The black SUV (GAV-001) remained parked there, abandoned. Much good it did me.

"Okay," said Leon, heading back inside. "I'm giving them one more week to collect these freaking boxes, and then I'm calling dibs on E.J.'s sewing machine."

"Will you look the other way while I pinch some of those sketch books?" I asked him.

"Hell, I'll help you pack them."

"That's it," I said to Trace when she picked me up from the side of the road with my sad cardboard box under one arm. Sisters are the best. "No more men. No more doing weird favours for hot men with sad eyes. I'm done."

"You had me at no more men," she said with a sad smile as she drove us towards the Southern Outlet. "Rich handed me divorce papers when he picked up Daisy tonight."

"Bastard. Would it be tactless to break out the bubbly?" My divorce, by the time it came through, was a matter of celebration rather than sadness — I'd burned through all my emotions on all the financial and legal betrayal, not to mention the terror of my arrest and trial. By the time we got around to addressing the marriage, I had no more *anything* to give. When I signed my papers, Trace and I demolished two bottles of really good champagne she had been gifted by a client... and I didn't even cry until the second bottle.

(We'd known her own divorce formalities were coming for a while now, I already had a couple of bottles stored in the fridge for this occasion.)

"Why not," said Trace. "If I'm going to weep over lost love, I might as well do it in style."

"That's my girl."

A text buzzed on my phone, from Paisley.

Check Chameleon's Insta RIGHT NOW omg

I swiped through to the app, which I rarely used, and searched for Chameleon's user account.

A video came up, shaky from someone's phone. I played it, while Trace drove us home. It was Meegan, her bright white and purple hair draped with one of the torn green veils I'd dyed. It must have been picked up from the beach, or the photoshoot trailer. She had a lopsided crown of flowers holding the veil in place, and her mascara was running. She looked drunk, or high, or both.

She wore the same green sleeveless shirt I remembered from the beach, but had lost a layer or two along the way; her shoulders were bare.

"I know you follow this account because you really care about Chameleon," Meegan slurred, pupils blown wide. The framing was slightly off, but you could see a fence line behind her when her hand swayed, and occasionally the corner of a building. "So I want to tell you about my friend E.J. He was just... kind and sweet and talented. So talented. No one will ever know how great he was. He made me a better artist. A better person." She started to cry, a bit of snot flying. "I really loved him. And I want to…"

She dropped the phone for a moment, giving us a view of blue sky and a very familiar hills hoist. Then she scrabbled for it, settled herself, and started talking again. "Don't trust them, any of you. Don't ask questions about who Chameleon is, or where they went. It's better that Chameleon doesn't exist any more. Don't trust his family. One of them killed him."

The video ended.

"Wow," said Trace. "Intense."

I hit the 'call' button to talk to Paisley.

"You saw it," they said instantly. I could tell Paisley was as rattled as I was, because they didn't immediately tease me for making a phone call instead of texting.

"Yeah, she does not look okay."

"And you saw…"

"Yep. Should we—?"

"I mean, yes. Obviously!"

"What?" said Trace impatiently. "Read me in, my kid is at her dad's and I have *nothing* going on this weekend."

"We'll pick you up in 15 and head over there together," I told Paisley and hung up. "The video was filmed in our backyard."

"*Our* backyard?"

"Fashionably Late's backyard," I corrected. "In front of the laundry. She had one of our veils, too — which I hope she snagged from the beach, otherwise we've had another break in."

Morgaine really was going to have to install those video cameras.

"You don't have to come," I told Trace.

"Oh no," she said determinedly. "You're not leaving me out. What else am I going to do on a Saturday night, drink champagne and cry over my divorce papers?"

"We can make time for that later," I promised.

I wasn't sure what we were going to find. It had still been daylight when Meegan filmed her video. When Trace, Paisley and I finally piled out of the car in front of the shop, it was nearly dark.

I saw Meegan's veil first. It was fluttering from one of the Hills Hoists, where it had snagged on a couple of pegs. The voile was tearing; another sharp breeze and it would slip away into the sky, flying around haphazardly until it wrapped itself around a chimney or a seagull.

"No one's broken in at the back," called Paisley, checking the back door and the studio window, while I retrieved the veil.

"Don't speak too soon," said Trace, looking up at the laundry shed. Normally you could see right in, through the glass frontage, but it was too dark right now. Nothing but shadows. Still, when Trace pointed the torch from her phone directly at the door, it was easy to see where someone had knocked through a panel of glass with a brick.

"Bloody hell. What even is the point of neighbours if they don't notice us being burgled," I grumbled. "Twice."

"There can't be much of value in there."

I shrugged. "Depends on how much you value quality dyes. There's hundreds of dollars of materials in the store cupboard, but no one's going to pawn them to buy a packet of cigarettes. The dryer might be worth a bit, I suppose. If you could get it out."

"There is that super valuable celebrity wedding dress," Paisley pointed out.

"We don't have that. We don't even know where it is."

"Nah, but we've been broken into twice since your mate with the shoulders started sniffing around, and a grand total of no times before that. Maybe someone thought we had the dress."

"I guess so," I mused. "If they broke into the shed the last time, they would have scored a few dresses at least. There's not much left for them now."

"This is where we call the police, right?" Paisley said thoughtfully.

"Yes," said Trace, giving me a sympathetic look. "This is when most people would call the police."

"It's not an emergency," I said quickly. "For all we know, Meegan chucked a brick after making her video. And it's a Saturday night, they're not going to prioritise something this small." This was a perfectly reasonable excuse.

"Morgaine can call Sergeant Torrance in the morning," said Paisley, cheering up at the thought of our local cop with his crush on our boss. "Arthurrrr. I'm sure he'll come running to play knights and robbers. Cops and dragons?"

"You'd better not be calling Morgaine a dragon." I climbed up the step to check on the door. "Maybe we can get some duct tape to fix this up temporarily? Bit of cardboard or something. We won't get a glazier in on a Sunday, so it has to last two days."

"Let me hold the light." Trace hopped up the steps behind me with her phone, as I pushed the busted door open. She swung it over my shoulder, letting the piercing beam of light skim the length of the long laundry room, with its four baths.

"Oh no," I breathed, panic prickling up inside me.

The bath at the end, the one still full of green dye in case there was an emergency veil situation I had to deal with. There was a shape sticking out of it, awkwardly. As I took a few steps closer, I realised that it looked more like two shapes. Two feet.

"Is someone sleeping in your bath," Trace whispered, on the edge of giggles.

"I don't think so," I said heavily

We got closer, and closer. Finally, I was standing over the bath.

Trace caught her breath, realising what I had figured out a minute ago. "Oh, no."

Behind us, Paisley switched on the lights. The fluoro beam overhead stuttered into life, and then blazed over our heads, illuminating the scene.

A dead woman lay submerged in the bath full of green dye, her hair floating over her face. It was white and purple once, her hair. But now, all we could see was green.

11

THERE WAS NO AVOIDING THE POLICE NOW. AS IT TURNS out, even on a Saturday night, they come *fast* when you report a dead body.

The next few hours were all about answering police questions, waiting around for more police to arrive, then more questions. My idea of hell, basically.

By the time we were allowed to go home, Trace and I didn't feel like cracking out the sparkling white any more, divorce or no divorce.

I was wrung out, still tensed for the possibility that I might be considered a suspect.

"Do not watch that video again," Trace said sternly when she saw my hand creeping towards my phone.

"She looked so miserable and scared," I murmured.

"And paranoid, and smashed. This isn't something you can fix, Sam."

That much was certainly true. Meegan Kelly had drowned in a bath of dye that I filled. There was nothing to be done to make that un-happen.

"First things first," said Trace, setting two cups of hot chocolate in front of us on Aunt Harriet's kitchen table. The mugs both had pictures of corgis on them, because Aunt Harriet was mad about corgis, and we continued to live in the shadow of everything she had owned. "I want you to look me in the eye and tell me there is absolutely zero per cent chance that this Donovan Hottie with the sunglasses and the sharp suit murdered that woman."

I stared at her. I drank some chocolate, to see if that made the night better. It did not, which is rare for a drink with this many melted marshmallows in it. "What on earth makes you think he was involved?"

"Um, let's see. He's had you running around looking for info on his dead brother, hunting some mythical dress for a pop star. Like that's even remotely believable. He must have been one of the last people to talk to Meegan, supposedly to arrange a meet-up at the Swoosh Hutch, but you only have his word for it. He acted super weird when his dad turned up and then he *ditched you* in town. Meegan said on her video not to trust his family, which has to include him, right? Also, he is like, stupidly good looking, you get all soft when you talk about him, and you haven't had sex in two years."

"That last part is information you do not need to have in your head." It had been longer than two years.

"And the rest of it?" said Trace. "Come on, Sam. Really think about it. I'm not looking to solve any crimes here, I just want to make sure you don't end up shagging a murderer."

She had a point, which was annoying. But these were

all factors I had already considered. "If I get soft about him, which I dispute, it's only because I feel sorry for him." And his stupid sad eyes.

"Exactly," said Trace. "*You feel sorry for him.* That is exactly how you end up on the seven o'clock news, saying 'I had no idea, he seemed so nice.' I'm looking out for you."

"Fine," I said, and went to grab a piece of Daisy's drawing paper and a Sharpie. Bright green, which was weirdly appropriate. "Let's work this out. The photo shoot finished up before five. Everyone started drifting off. Donovan asked me to go meet Meegan with him. I dropped the veils back at Fashionably Late…"

"At the laundry shed?" Trace interrupted.

"No, in the shop. I didn't go around the back. Donovan and I drove into town together. We were at the Swoosh Hutch for a while, waiting for Meegan before Leon turned up — he was expecting her too, said he'd lost track of her but got a text. Talked to him for a while, unpacked some boxes, and then… I guess it was about six thirty when GAZ-001 turned up and Donovan ditched me. It was starting to get properly dark."

"Wait," said Trace, and checked her phone. "6:37, your call to me. How long did you wait before calling?"

"Like, three minutes. Five?" I had to collect something from E.J. 'Chameleon' Brady's boxes first. It hadn't taken long — I'm efficient when I'm annoyed.

"That's good." Trace took the Sharpie off me and made a few notes. "So Donovan and/or his dad could have gone straight to Fashionably Late, drowned her in the bath, and been home in time for Marple before we turned up and found her."

"You think they killed her together? They left together." I wondered at what point Donovan had gone back to fetch the other car… and whether at any point he felt guilty about leaving me stranded.

"Father and son bonding experience? It would help if we knew whether or not they were each other's alibi."

"I'm pretty sure the police think she was killed earlier. When the forensics team turned up at the shop, I heard one of them calling out that she was cold. We found her, what, between 7:30 and 8? The police were there by 8:30 or so. How long does it even take for a body to go cold?"

Obviously it didn't help that she'd been lying in a cold bath.

"I don't know, Sam, that didn't come up in my real estate training course." Trace frowned, looking at the timeline. "When did you last see Meegan alive?"

"Threeish? Three-thirtyish. When Donovan went over to talk to her, during the beach shoot."

"Did you always have eyes on him after that?"

"No, because I am not stalking him." I had a sudden visual memory of him popping out from behind that trailer. "Wait, when did that video go up on Instagram?"

Trace waved her hand in a circle at me until I had opened the app. It took a little while to search for it. There were… a lot of comments.

"5:05," I said. "Okay. I was with him then. There isn't a window."

"Unless he and his dad did it later as a father-son bonding experience."

"There isn't a realistic window. I don't believe they were capable of teaming up on any project without screaming at each other. They'd have had to do it pretty fast and clear out before we got to her, if they were only half an hour ahead of us. And even in a bath of dye, she wouldn't have, you know..." Gone cold. The thought was horrible.

"Was he wearing a shirt?" Trace asked, interrupting my thoughts.

"What?"

"On the day, you know. He's been borrowing his brother's car, maybe he borrowed a shirt."

"Black t-shirt," I said confidently. "Under the suit jacket."

"You sure?"

"It was very tight. I noticed."

"Fine," said Trace, as if this was a great disappointment to her. "I'm convinced. You can sleep with him."

"I'm not going to sleep with him!" I protested.

She batted her eyelashes at me. "Are you sure, Sam? You can't afford to be picky. There aren't many tall, dark and handsome guys out there our age who are unmarried and almost certainly not a murderer."

"I'm going to bed," I told her, very pointedly.

The thing about Trace is she has a brain for organisation. We make a good team when we're not rubbing each other up the wrong way. I have considered, many times, how life might have turned out differently if I started my wedding planner business with her and not my husband.

If we had to team up and do a murder, Trace and I would definitely be more efficient at it than Donovan and his aggro dad.

Another thing about Trace is when she gets a bee in her bonnet about something, there's no stopping her.

So, I shouldn't have been surprised when I got up early the next morning and found several whiteboards propped up around Aunt Harriet's kitchen, detailing much of what had happened to me over the last few days, across several tidy lists.

"What is this?" I said blankly. "And also, good morning?"

"Okay," said Trace, popping up from behind the cupboards with a bowl of cereal and a handful of washable markers. "Suspects list. Do you think I've missed anyone out?"

I looked at the suspect list. "Where you say high school bitch, I presume you mean Jeena Harding-Brady?"

"Jeena! I knew it had a J in it." She made her correction.

"And I don't know who Sparkle Pony is." I paused, thinking about it. "Do you mean Harper Park?"

"Got it." More writing.

"You remembered Leon's name, I see."

"It's a nice name, it was on our boys' list when Daisy was born."

"Trace. What are you doing?" I looked more closely. "Why am I on the suspect list?"

She pointed her marker at me. "You found the body, Sam. It's suspicious."

I knew she was joking, but the very thought of being suspected was kind of traumatising. "I notice you're not on the list!"

"I ran out of room. And also, I know I didn't do it." Trace surveyed her handiwork with pride. "I borrowed these whiteboards from work, they were having a chuck out. We are going to solve this."

"Why would we do that? It's a job for the police." Normal people trust the police to handle murder inquiries. Normal people assume that police don't arrest people without a very good reason.

Trace made a scoffing sound. "The police. They probably think *you* did it."

"That is not helpful or comforting," I snapped back, even if it did reflect my deepest fears about this whole scenario.

Trace gave me a mildly sympathetic look, and wrote a question mark next to my name on the suspect list. "You're a red herring."

"Good to know."

"Tell me more about Meegan. She doesn't give a lot of personal detail away on her Instagram."

"I don't know much."

"Husband, boyfriend? Murder is almost always the husband or the boyfriend. Which is a depressing fact to learn at 8am on a Sunday, but I've been doing a lot of internet research while feeling cynical about my failed marriage."

"The only relationship I sort of know about is E.J. Ethan Brady. And no one's actually confirmed they were together. Jeena thought they were. I think Donovan thought that too." I paused. "Yeah no, pretty sure Leon confirmed it."

"Ethan's dead so he can't have drowned her in the bath yesterday," Trace mused. "Unless he's a special category of criminal genius." She tapped the top of her suspects list where the names Gavin Brady, Donovan Brady and Jeena Harding-Brady were displayed. Next to Donovan's name Trace had written the words 'probably not' and what looked like the side-eye emoji. "Comes back to these three, doesn't it? The family Meegan said we shouldn't trust."

That was hard to argue with. Even (especially?) if two of them were each other's alibis.

"I hate this," I told Trace.

She gave me a very firm look. The same look that she had on her face when she told me she wanted me to move in with her, and when she told me it was over with her and Rich. The same look she had on her face when she told me 'none of this is your fault' after I found out what my husband had done.

I've always found it reassuring, when Trace gets firm about things.

"This is going to make you miserable," she told me. "And stressed out, until it's over. We're going to take control in the only way we can, and get this murder solved so it's not hanging over your head any more. Right?"

My sister. She knew me so well.

"Yeah," I said, a whole lot less reluctant. "You're right. Let's do this."

I was arrested on a Sunday morning.

Nearly two years ago, two plain clothes detectives (are there any other kind?) turned up on my doorstep and informed me of my rights. It took them six days to put a case together, after I first reported that my husband and a large sum of money from our shared business account had both disappeared.

It never occurred to me, when I originally called in the police, how guilty the whole thing would make me look.

The police case against me rested largely on the fact that I had not seen my then-husband for 72 hours before I made that call, and had sent no texts or emails to him (or attempted to contact him) during that period. That 72 hours gave Malcolm ample time to clear our future fund (deposits paid by clients towards upcoming wedding events), and hop not only on to a plane out of Hobart, but a connecting flight to Bali, leaving the country.

It looked, I realised in retrospect, pretty damn suspicious. Even after it became evident that Abby, our PA, had left with him.

Those two calm, polite detectives asked me over and over — why didn't I try to get in touch with him? How could I possibly not have known or cared where my husband was? Was he in the habit of disappearing for days? Had we had a fight?

The truth was, I was tired. Tired of Mal, tired of being

let down. Physically and emotionally exhausted. But when you've spent a whole marriage not saying that sort of thing out loud (because everything's fine, and you're a successful couple, and you have your dream business, and things will get easier next year), your first instinct is not to explain your motivations openly to complete strangers.

Turns out even after you realise you *should have* explained yourself from the start, it's hard to do that in a way that looks honest and open. Because of course, you're still hiding details, even from yourself. Pride looks a lot like guilt, to someone looking for guilt.

To this day, I'm not 100% certain what my thinking process was during those 72 hours, when Malcolm didn't come home and I didn't know yet how badly he'd screwed me over. I remember being upset that he only told me at the last minute he wouldn't be able to help with the Taylor-Taylor wedding (bride and groom, both with the first name of Taylor, adorable) so I had to scramble to bring in relief staff. I was flat out for most of Friday and Saturday, co-ordinating every step of the wedding on my own, picking up all Mal's dropped balls. When it was over, I came home and slept.

Sure, he wasn't in my bed for the second night running, but given that I was still so pissed off at him, I was almost relieved.

That Sunday, I forgot I had a husband. I slept late, ate what I wanted, took a long bath, tidied up. Watched some old episodes of *A Country Practice* because streaming nostalgia TV is a blessing. I slowly, slowly got my brain back. It was the best weekend I'd had in years.

I didn't think of him as missing. I assumed he was

staying out of my way to avoid a fight. Maybe he was at his Mum's, or a friend's. I. Didn't. Care.

I painted my nails. I read a couple of chapters of a book. I napped. When I thought of him at all, it was with a sinking feeling that I quickly repressed. The truth was I didn't want him to come home. I didn't need to know where he was.

(The thought of splitting up permanently crossed my mind that weekend, but what would that achieve? How would it work? Our whole lives were wrapped up in each other, home and business. Bank accounts. Loans. I couldn't imagine how to begin unravelling it all. Joke was on me because as it turned out, he'd put quite a bit of thought into how to end our marriage.)

On Monday, I went into the office and carried on as well as I could. Abby not turning up for work that day was more of an inconvenience than Mal's disappearing act. I answered emails and phone calls. Tidied up a few loose ends. And then, four hours into my work day, I noticed the missing money. I called Mal to see if he knew what was going on — he handled the finances, after all. Surely it was some kind of mistake. Had he moved the money to a new account without mentioning it?

Looking back, I can see why people thought my story had holes so wide you could drive through them. I wouldn't have believed me, if I wasn't me. By the time the detectives decided to arrest me, six days after I reported the missing money (and belatedly, my missing husband), I was in a haze of shock and denial. I barely believed the events of the previous week myself.

I spent a day and a half in police custody after my

arrest. Rich bailed me out — he and Trace were still together, at the time, and I was relieved to have a wealthy brother-in-law to make that part, at least, slightly less horrible than it could have been. (It was pretty horrible, I don't recommend it.)

People never believe me when I tell them that the trial, and what came after the trial, was even worse than being arrested. Partly that's because it lasted longer... a long tail of public humiliation, vs a short, numbing period of shock and isolation.

The ongoing stress and horror of having a sword hanging over my head. The anxiety about speaking in public, of trying to clear my name. The possibility that they might find me guilty and I would have to go to jail for real.

Months of uncertainty, of absorbing my losses, of fear. The hits kept coming.

By the time I was able to talk about it with any clarity, I was used to people not believing me. My circle of trust and support had shrunk so tightly that I found it very hard to talk to people at all.

This is all a long way of saying that, shortly before lunchtime on the Sunday after we found Meegan's body in the dye tub, the last thing I was emotionally prepared for was two quietly-spoken plain-clothes detectives, standing on my doorstep. Especially as one of them was very familiar to me.

"Detective Inspector Rosenthal," I said faintly.

The small, quiet man nodded. He wasn't surprised I remembered him. "Ms Sullivan. It's been a while. Do you mind if we ask you a few questions?"

Did. I. Mind.

"Not at all," I said, forcing a smile. "Come on in."

I had nothing to hide. Right?

12

I LED THE DETECTIVES INTO AUNT HARRIET'S LIVING
room, with its layers of quilts and embroidered throw
cushions, lace curtains, teapot collection. I'd never been
quite so aware of how different this place was to the last
home I had. When Detective Inspector Rosenthal arrested
me, I lived in a bright and modern house near the city, all
magazine-shiny and matching. Fashionable, sleek, staged.

He probably had no thoughts at all about where I lived
now. I was sure he was above such things. Detective
Inspector Rosenthal liked truth, logic, and stories that
made perfect sense when fitted together.

Even now I could see him glancing around the room,
trying to put our jumble of comfort together like it was a
jigsaw puzzle.

Trace popped her head out of the kitchen. "Who
was — oh."

"Tracy Madison?" said Detective Rosenthal to confirm
her identity. Like she hadn't given testimony for my
defence.

She gave him her professional real estate agent smile which instantly made her look far more mature, even though she was wearing a Star Wars t-shirt and trackies. "Tracy Sullivan now, I got divorced recently. Inspector Rosenthal. How nice. I'll put the kettle on, shall I?"

"That would be very kind."

No, wait. That wasn't her real estate agent smile. She was *sparkling*. That was her interesting man has walked into the room smile. Hadn't seen that one in a while.

What even was happening here? I glanced at the second officer, a tall man whose name I hadn't taken in. He looked neutral, which was unhelpful. Unless it meant… the police really were only here to ask a few questions?

I tried to settle my pulse. Detective Inspector Rosenthal probably wouldn't drink a cup of my sister's tea and then arrest me. (He'd refused refreshments last time, and the quiet plain clothes officer at his side had barely even made eye contact with me.) My pulse was not accepting logical arguments today.

By the time we were all sorted out with tea and/or coffee, I was at least able to fake being chill. Luckily, I wasn't expected to lead the conversation. Trace, knowing I must be freaking out, took on 90% of the 'helping with inquiries' load.

It involved a lot more sparkling than was strictly necessary.

Trace explained the Instagram video and how we came to find Meegan in the bath, all details we had shared with Sergeant Torrance and the other police officers on the scene the night before.

"This is the second recent break-in at your place of

work," Rosenthal observed, looking directly at me. "The clothes shop."

"Yes," I said quietly. Diana would instantly correct the man about Fashionably Late being a boutique, not a mere shop, but I wasn't feeling Diana Wave levels of confidence right now.

"Do you have reason to believe Meegan Kelly was also responsible for the first break-in?"

Odd question. I thought about it, my natural curiosity taking over my ingrained fear of saying the wrong thing to police officers, and this detective in particular. "I'm not sure. I only met her a couple of days ago."

"The break-in was after the incident with the wedding dresses."

"There have been a lot of incidents with wedding dresses this week," I said. "Can you be more specific?"

Rosenthal gave me a tired sort of look. "Do you know anyone who wished Miss Kelly harm?"

"I barely knew her."

"You were asking questions about her, on your visit to the…" He checked his notebook. "Swoosh Hutch."

"My interest was purely dress related." I had learned my lesson. Explain your feelings, Sam. Provide emotional context where possible. "I felt bad about the whole wedding dress… thing. Dyeing, them, I mean. And there was still a valuable dress missing at that point. If the Bradys wanted to make a big deal about that, it wouldn't be good for our business."

"Ah yes," said Inspector Rosenthal, putting his note-book down. "Explain your connection to Donovan Brady."

"I don't have one," I said immediately. "We knew each

other vaguely at school, but he didn't even remember me when we met again recently. I know his sister-in-law, Jeena. But we hadn't seen each other in years when I bought the dresses off her."

"You have been seen in Mr Brady's company a great deal lately."

Did it make Donovan look more or less suspicious, to be hanging out with me? My taste in men is infamously terrible.

"Still all dress-related," I said, managing somehow not to sound like I was biting into a lemon. *Relax, Sam. Nothing to hide. Be an open book.*

The Inspector nodded thoughtfully. "Tell me more about the recent dress incidents."

"Which one?"

"All of them." He positioned his pen over his note-book, ready to write. "From the beginning."

By the time Inspector Rosenthal left (without arresting me, score!), he had managed to draw out pretty much every detail of what had happened to me ever since I first drove up to Jeena Harding-Brady's house on the day of Ethan's funeral.

I felt emptied out but also, weirdly light. "Is it me?" I said to Trace after he was gone. "Or did that feel like he didn't suspect me at all?"

"Why would he suspect you?" she asked airily, as if she hadn't personally added my name to her whiteboard. (Thank goodness she took the opportunity to turn those facing the other way when she ducked into the kitchen.) "You're not involved with the Brady family. You don't have a motive to kill Meegan. Unless you secretly stole that pop star's wedding dress and you're looking to sell it on the black market, I reckon we're in the clear."

I looked at her in horror. "I'm so glad you didn't say that when he was here! And speaking of detectives..."

"No, I think we're done with this conversation," she said quickly.

"Were you *flirting* with him?"

"Only a bit."

"Tracy Annette, I am shocked! That man is old enough to be your..." Well, not father. It was hard to tell, really. So much bland, so few age cues. "Inappropriate lit professor?"

She smacked my arm. "Shut up, I never shamed you about your teacher crushes. And yes, I flirted. I thought it might distract him from paying attention to you, since you looked like you were about to melt through the floor."

"I mean, he did arrest me," I mumbled.

"*One* time."

"It only takes one time! It was traumatising. Most people go their whole lives without being wrongfully arrested."

Trace started tidying away the cups to the kitchen. "Rosenthal was pretty nice, actually. Low key. I wonder if that means he already knows who did it."

"With most murders, the police already know who did it, the hard part is proving it." I read that once.

Trace glanced at me over her shoulder, knowing

exactly what I was thinking. "Except when they get it wrong."

"Except when they get it wrong," I agreed.

We were allowed to open Fashionably Late on Monday, despite the backyard being taped off as a crime scene. The body of Meegan Kelly had been removed, of course. We were asked to avoid the laundry shed for a few more days, as the investigation proceeded.

Morgaine sensibly called both me and Paisley in, because the shop was jamming all day. Most of the customers were locals, hungry for the gossip. Carol from the gift shop came by three times.

After school let out, we attracted clusters of teen girls, mostly stationed outside on the pavement or across the road by the steps to the beach, staring and taking pictures with their phone.

"Anyone would think that a celebrity died in our bath," complained Morgaine.

"I mean…" I said thoughtfully. "Chameleon had nearly a million followers on Instagram."

"And thanks to that video on Saturday, everyone thinks Meegan Kelly was Chameleon," Paisley added.

At what point do you count as an official celebrity? I'd go with the definition of 'people who have never met you have a lot of feelings about your death.' Chameleon qualified.

By the next day, the teenagers weren't even bothering with school. They set up their staring stations before we opened for the day. Some of them brought flowers and candles like they were holding a vigil, only less well organised. By now, word must have spread about how Meegan died, because the girls started turning up in green items of clothing — random hats, shirts and socks at first, but after a while they were all wearing the same straggly green scarves and arm bands. Home-dyed merch? You had to admire their tenacity.

The police still had the driveway next to our shop taped up, and occasionally had a couple of uniformed officers roll past in their car. They ordered the teenagers in green to stop loitering more than once, but the teens would just scatter and come back half an hour later.

Whenever our backs were turned, more flowers piled up in front of the shop, and in the driveway under the police tape. We blew out any candles left behind if they were lit, but otherwise let it happen on the grounds that there were more of them than of us. Also, as long as there were forty or so teenagers observing our shop, we were unlikely to have further unexpected break-ins, or dead bodies dumped here.

Morgaine spent a lot of the day frowning at her own phone, which made a change from frowning at the customers.

"You're not trying to figure out Instagram, are you?" Paisley asked finally. "You know the over 40s get a free pass on learning any form of social media, right?"

"Hilarious," said Morgaine. "I'm worried about my sister. She's been sending me cryptic messages about big things coming that might affect the shop. Can't figure out if she means my shop or her shop."

I mean, it was Vivi. She was never going to be interested in anyone else's shop.

"Sisters can be weird," I said helpfully. "Mine, for instance, has been flirting with police inspectors and making charts to figure out if men I spend time with are secretly murderers."

"Maybe Vivi's going to change her shop's name from Bridezillion to something that doesn't make women feel bad about themselves," considered Morgaine.

"You wish," said Paisley. They leaned into the window display, eyeing the flocks of teens who were pretending not to stare across the road at us. "Do you think when all this is over, it would be tasteless to charge for tours of our laundry shed?"

"Yes it would," I said immediately. "Extremely tasteless."

"What if I charged for them to have the authentic experience of doing our laundry for us?"

I hesitated. "Also tasteless, but you're starting to sell me on it."

The doorbell jangled, and we all looked up.

Leon and Harper from the Swoosh Hutch stood framed in our doorway, dressed as if they were about to star in a music video about a dramatic goth funeral.

Harper wore a black tutu over candy-striped tights, her hair in pig-tails and a black pillbox hat with a tiny black net veil. She was holding the world's largest floral wreath (also in pink and black) and every inch of her skin that was showing was smeared in glitter. She looked like she had been crying but also like she had put her makeup on that day in order to cry messily through it, and then take a lot of sad panda Instagram pictures of herself.

Leon looked equally dramatic, in a black vest over a ripped white shirt and his black bat jeans. He had dark glitter in his hair, and he looked like… well, clearly whoever had done Harper's makeup had also done his, with a lot more deliberate smearing of eyeliner.

"We've come to pay our respects," he said stiffly, as if expecting us to laugh.

Harper just glared, daring us all not to take her seriously.

Morgaine looked about two seconds away from kicking them out. Paisley quickly jumped in.

"It's okay, we know them. This is Leon and Harper, they uh. They were friends with Meegan. Actual friends, not random stalkers."

Morgaine sighed. "Fine. Police have requested that we not cross the tape but you can go through as far as the back steps."

We went through the kitchen at the back rather than lead Leon and Harper through the studio, which was for the best. Glitter in the teabags and biscuits was one thing, but glitter in the sewing machines would be impossible to undo.

Harper immediately made a beeline for the steps leading up to the laundry shed, which had a line of police tape still across them. Very pointedly, she placed her wreath directly in front of the steps and then started taking pictures of it with her phone.

"I know this is a hassle," said Leon, sounding exhausted. "But it was this or watch her throw cans of paint at a yard full of very expensive electric cars, and I thought this was less likely to get her arrested."

Harper was now taking a series of angry and dramatic selfies with the police tape and the Hills Hoists clearly in the background. I watched her move around until she found what must have been the same spot where Meegan recorded her video, and then started recording one of her own.

"I hope this doesn't come back to bite us," said Paisley thoughtfully, and promptly wandered over to join Harper. "Want me to hold the phone for you, or are you happy with the DIY effect?"

Leon leaned his head against our kitchen door, looking wrecked.

"Sorry for your loss," I offered.

"Thanks. It sucks. First E.J., then Meegan. And now we're losing the Swoosh Hutch too."

"Why?"

Leon looked grim. "You know how E.J.'s aggro dad is a big deal? Now he's out to ruin us. Didn't like the news that his son was into girly stuff like fashion, is the polite way of putting it. The media have connected Meegan's death to E.J.'s, building it up as this whole sinister fashion scandal or whatever. So, the stories about the sporty car empire family have been replaced with frock drama. And good old Gavin Brady is blaming it all on us."

"I take it he wasn't polite about his disapproval," I said steadily.

"Nope. We got a phone call from him yesterday, spewing all kinds of homophobic bullshit about us turning his son into... well, you get it. *Fairy clothes horse* was one of the nicer phrases he used. Last night, someone chucked bricks through two of the studio's windows and sprayed slurs all over the outside walls."

"That's horrible." The more I learned about Gavin Brady, the less I liked him.

"Oh, it gets better," said Leon. "Today we got a call from our landlord. He's blaming us for the damage done to the heritage stained glass, and he's using it as an excuse to evict us."

"Your super chill landlord who didn't mind you plumbing a sink into a church?"

Leon gave a stiff-shouldered shrug. "Turns out he belongs to the same club as Gavin bloody Brady, and doesn't want to make waves. He claims there have been noise complaints from our neighbours for months but this is the first we've heard of it. We sunk so much of our own money into the refit of the church hall, all the crowd-funding loot is gone — oh and Meegan was hiding bills from us, which explains why she was so hot to get a new studio member the second E.J. died. We're in debt up to our necks. So, that's it. Out on our ear with a trailer-load of sewing equipment. No more Swoosh Hutch."

"And that's why Harper wanted to throw paint cans at the Brady car yard," I said thoughtfully. I was feeling a lot more sympathetic to Harper. If melodramatic goth selfies and glitter makeup helped get her through the next few days, I would hold her beer.

"I had to talk her down from paint bombs! But, yeah." Leon fidgeted with his wrist, where he had a bright green tattoo peeking out from under his sleeve. A frog, I realised. It was weirdly familiar, and I remembered seeing a version of the same artwork on denim, in one of the photos displayed in his studio.

Lizards are a lot like frogs, when you think about it.

"Chameleon," I said softly. "Funny name for a designer. Why be anonymous?"

Leon's shoulders had stiffened. "People have their own reasons for hiding," he said, as if he was trying to sound light. "I always thought it was a pretty cool name to use as a clothing brand. Because of my name, you know?"

I didn't have to be a cryptic crossword lover like Aunt Harriet to spot the 'leon' in Chameleon.

"What happened?"

He shrugged, covering up his wrist with a sleeve. "Someone beat me to it. You know the fashion industry. Ruthless."

"Someone stole your idea?"

He shrugged again, looking carefully neutral.

My phone rang, from an unknown number. I stared at it for a moment, remembering that I never had managed to collect Donovan Brady's phone number. Could it be him?

"Leon!" Harper yelled. "Come over here so I can take a picture of you looking sad. If we're gonna make a Go Fund Me work, we need epic tragedy with eyeliner."

Leon loped over in her direction, leaving me to my

mystery phone call. And, coincidentally I'm sure, avoiding any further questions I had.

"Hello?"

"Ms Sullivan," said a voice that still gave me chills, even (especially) when he was being terribly polite. "This is Detective Inspector Rosenthal. I have some further questions for you, if you can spare time for a meeting."

I knew his suspicious lack of suspicion was too good to be true. And this time I didn't have Trace to protect me.

13

IT WAS POSSIBLE THAT SOMEDAY I WOULD BE ABLE TO hold a conversation with Detective Inspector Rosenthal without constantly being terrified he was about to arrest me and throw my life into a downward spiral, all over again.

This was not that day.

"What did you want to talk about?" I asked, proud of myself for sounding professional and not at all like I was on the verge of tears.

"I'd rather discuss this in person. I assume you'd rather not come into the station?"

Considerate of him.

"No, I mean yes. I'd rather not." I looked around. Harper had put her veiled hat on Leon and was attempting to arrange him in some kind of pose like he was in a coffin. Paisley was playing assistant director. "It's — quite chaotic here at the shop."

He did not need to see this particular scene.

We compromised on the duck park, since it was directly opposite my house but not actually in my house.

Close enough that, if he didn't actually arrest me, I could immediately go home and cry into a hot bath from the stress of thinking that he might.

When I told Morgaine why I needed to leave early, she gave me a steady look, then made me take off the over-sized cotton shirt I'd been wearing as my top layer. (Spring in Tasmania is all about the layers, especially this far south when we get all the weather at once.) She handed me a soft, deep purple garment with a peacock feather design. It was cut nicely, all swing and pockets, and made me feel about two inches taller.

"One of Diana's designs," Morgaine said with a brief smile, straightening my lapels. "She calls it Confidence."

"I can always do with some of that."

There's something calming about a duck park. Nothing bad can happen there, except of course, people feeding the wrong things to the ducks (don't give them bread), and teenagers haranguing passers by for feeding the wrong things to the ducks (don't give them *bread*).

With Aunt Harriet's little house facing the park directly, Trace and I felt a sort of ownership of the ducks. I think everyone along our street felt the same way. It was a space that belonged to all of us.

Detective Inspector Rosenthal joined me on the park bench. "Grapes?" he said, raising his eyebrows slightly.

"The local teens have many opinions about what is and is not appropriate food for ducks," I informed him, biting a grape in half and throwing it to the nearest duck, who would clearly protect me from the police if necessary. "Oats are fine, and cooked rice, but random park-goers get weird about you throwing globs of cooked rice around in a park. Grapes work, but you can't give them whole ones or they might choke." I threw another split grape. It was something to do with my hands. "What did you want to ask me?" Hooray, my voice didn't shake at all.

"I was hoping for your expert opinion," Rosenthal said.

That was not what I had been expecting. I gave him an incredulous look. "What is it you think I'm an expert at?"

Weddings. Fraudulent husbands. Wrongful arrest. Ducks.

"Green dye," he said calmly.

Ah. Well. Yes. Got me there.

"Go on," I said.

Rosenthal drew a buff yellow envelope out of his jacket and showed me a couple of glossy photographs. "I realise this isn't ideal for our purpose, but I can't take evidence out of the police station."

I looked at the pictures carefully. I could see a man's shirt: good quality but basic. White with a pin-stripe. Probably far more expensive than I could possibly guess. I couldn't pick the designer but I was certain it was in the category where I'd recognise the label. One of the photos showed a close up of a sleeve.

There was green dye all over this side of the shirt: clotted at the cuff, and splashed in little flicks almost up to the elbow. From the larger picture, you could also see splashes up the front of the shirt.

"Needless to say," said Inspector Rosenthal. "This is confidential. I'd appreciate your discretion."

"Yes, I can see why." You didn't have to be an expert in dye. One look at these pictures and anyone's first thought would be that the man wearing this shirt was the same one who shoved Meegan Kelly into a green bath. "I don't actually know how she died? Technically, I mean."

To my surprise, he went ahead and told me. "We don't have a clear picture of that currently. She inhaled water and dye, so she was alive when she went underwater. A small bruise on the back of her head. Either she was pushed, and didn't come back up... or she fell on her own. There was water on the floor, and she was inebriated. It's possible she slipped."

"No," I said. "There wasn't water on the floor. Not when I left the bath. Those tiles are washable, but I still wouldn't have left dye water on the ground, I'd have cleaned it up right away. It felt weird to leave the bath with dye in it for so long, and I only did it so we could colour match the wedding veils if we needed more for the photo shoot. The floor was clean and dry when I locked up the shed on Friday night, and again when I collected the dyed items on Saturday before we drove out to the goat farm."

"Interesting," said Inspector Rosenthal.

"You think whoever wore this shirt held her under the water until she drowned?" You might get this amount of splash for merely pushing her in, but I doubted it.

"It's a possibility," he said, not giving anything away.

"I still don't see how I can help."

"You've been very helpful already. But in fact, what I wanted to ask was whether, in your expert opinion, this shirt was stained with the same batch of dye that was in your bath at the shop?"

I frowned at the picture. "I mean, isn't it obvious?"

"It's an obvious conclusion to draw. But as I have learned over the course of my career, the obvious conclusion isn't always the right one." There was an odd note in his voice. Almost apologetic.

I met his eyes. "Can't you test it? To see if it's the same? The bath has been let out by now, I assume, but we have plenty of examples of fabric that was dyed from that batch."

"I can indeed test it. But the turnaround for that kind of testing is about six weeks. And I'd rather know the answer now, even if we can't prove it until later."

I looked back at the picture. "It's similar, but I can't swear it's the same. The same dye batch turns out differently on every fabric. Even the same fabric, if it's done under different conditions. Kept in sunlight or darkness, temperature, whether it's the first dip or the tenth. Even harder trying to figure this out from a photograph."

"And if you saw the shirt in person?" I'd known he was going to say that. If anything, I respected the fact that he'd held out so long.

I sighed. "Fine. Come on, then. Take me to the police station."

Expert dye witness had to be better than suspected fraud, surely.

~

I didn't live in Kingston Beach, back when I was arrested.
I was taken to a big, bustling station in the city, and kept in
a holding cell overnight until my bail was sorted.

If it was the same station, I probably couldn't have
forced myself to go back, expert dye witness or no expert
dye witness. But the Kingston station was a small town
building, all lemon yellow inside. More of a community
centre than a lock-up. I could do this.

The Inspector led me up a flight of stairs to his office.
Someone made me a cup of tea while we were waiting for
the Evidence team to release the shirt into his custody.
Turns out police stations are super friendly places if you're
not actually under arrest. I would probably appreciate that
later, when I was home and safe, but I was still awash with
tension.

At least I was wearing Diana Wave's Confidence,
wrapped in bright purple over my faded jeans and comfy
sneakers. Diana Wave would not be intimidated.

When it came down to it, Meegan Kelly had died in
my dye bath, and I did feel kind of responsible. *Suck it up,
Sam. Drink your polite cup of tea. Get the job done.*

When the shirt was brought out for me to examine, I
noticed right away something that had not been obvious in
the pictures. "Oh. That's really interesting."

Rosenthal's head came up like an alert doberman.
"What is it?"

"This shirt has been washed."

"Since the dye stains?"

"Definitely since the dye stains."

"What makes you say that?"

I pointed to the sleeve where the dye was heaviest, careful not to touch it. I would not be adding any DNA to their evidence pool, thank you very much. "See how the colour has bled into the fabric? It's softer than it would be if it had been recently splashed with dye and just left. You always rinse garments in cold after dyeing them, to set the colour and get rid of any excess. If you don't, whoever buys the thing ends up turning all their underwear green the first time they wash it."

"Proper wash, in a machine? Or rinsed under a tap?"

I considered, examining all the stains. "I can't say for sure, but looking at how it's bled at the edges, I'd say it was done with hot water. Which is not what you do to set dye — I guess it's what you do if you're hoping you can get rid of it. Assuming you have no idea how dye works. Does that help?"

"I'm not sure if 'help' is the right word," said Inspector Rosenthal, looking troubled. "I'd say you just made my job more complicated. Is it possible someone used the machines in your laundry shed to wash this?"

I shrugged. "If your people would let us back into the shed I guess I could see if the usual settings have been changed. We use hot water when washing older clothes, but never after dyeing. If you have fancy forensics people, they might find tiny fragments of green dye inside which- ever washing machine was used. But you'd have to be quick, before more loads get put through."

"Oh," said Inspector Rosenthal, looking like he had

been hit over the head. "I take it back, Ms Sullivan. You've just made my job much, much easier."

It was by far the most positive interaction I'd ever had with a police officer, and I really didn't know how to feel about it.

14

"YOUR SUIT'S BACK," OBSERVED PAISLEY THE NEXT
morning when I brought them a cup of tea from the
kitchen.

I glanced around the shop. "Do I have a suit?"

Paisley was wearing a bright striped waistcoat over a
tailored shirt, so if anyone was wearing a suit…

"Not that kind of suit. I mean bloke with the shoulders." Paisley pointed out the front window, past the
current display (Spring Retro, all hats, brights and
flowers).

Across the road, I could see Donovan Brady slouched
on a bench with his back to us, facing the beach. The clusters of teen girls in green scarves who still hovered nearby
kept eyeing him suspiciously, like they thought he might
be about to arrest them for being over dramatic.

"Does it count as stalking if he's facing in the other
direction?" I mused.

"There's only one way to find out…" teased Paisley.

I could have ignored Donovan. Of course I could. But

he was just sitting there, not moving. He didn't turn to look at the shop, or try to catch my attention just… sat.

"Fine," I muttered after half an hour of this. "I'm taking my break. But I'm only going over because you're curious."

"Whatever you want to tell yourself!" Paisley called after me, laughing.

~

"Fancy seeing you here," I said, sitting down on the other end of Donovan's bench.

He glanced up and gave me a brief smile, then returned his gaze to the beach where a young woman in a bright pink tracksuit was jogging across the sand. Her dark hair was scraped back into a scrunchie, and she looked like she had been going at it for some time.

He glanced around from time to time, taking in the general area, but was never far from having eyes on her.

Not moping or stalking at all, I realised belatedly. Certainly not trying to passive-aggressively get my attention. He was working.

"Is that Colette Cray?" I asked, not quite believing it.

I'd seen her on magazine covers, of course, though pop music generally passes me by. Trace and I had gone to see *A Midsummer Night's Dream* together, but Colette's Titania was all teased hair and goth makeup: fierce fairy glamour.

Today, she looked like a normal person. No one gave her a second look, which was impressive considering how many teen girls were lingering in the area. If they had strong feelings about Chameleon's instagram feed, chances were they represented a solid core of Colette Cray's fan demographic.

"She flew in last night," Donovan confirmed. "Beach jogging is this month's on-trend exercise. Speaking as her security detail, I prefer a treadmill, in a space with walls."

"Any sign of her wedding dress?"

"Not yet. We have a promising lead we're following up after this." He glanced over at me. "Sorry about the other day. Ditching you at the Swoosh Hutch. I don't always make rational decisions when my dad's around. I didn't even remember you until we were halfway back to his place."

"It's fine," I said. It wasn't fine (*didn't even remember you, just what every girl loves to hear*) but I found myself minding less after everything that happened since. "I suppose you heard about how we found Meegan?"

I hadn't paid much attention to the media coverage of her death, since most of my information comes directly from the local gossip network.

Donovan winced. "About that. They arrested Jeena this morning."

"Jeena?" I was momentarily stunned. "Wow. For killing Meegan?"

She had been at the beach that day. I remembered seeing Jeena briefly, complaining to Donovan. She'd driven off, but could have parked a few blocks away, and walked back to watch the fashion shoot like everyone else. Could she really have followed Meegan into the yard and...

"She was wearing a white dress," I said suddenly. I had

a strong visual memory of it, a svelte little mini dress in blinding white fabric. Something most people would never dare wear, because even a stray slice of cucumber would stain it forever… "Do the police seriously think she shoved someone in a bath full of green dye while wearing a white dress?"

"They believe she was wearing one of Ethan's old shirts, a button up," said Donovan glumly. "He wore big sizes, it would have covered most of the dress. They took like, swabs from her washing machine to prove she washed it at her house after it was splashed with dye…"

Oh, hell. Let Jeena Harding-Brady never find out it was me who made that suggestion to the police.

"How did the police get the shirt in the first place?" I hadn't asked Rosenthal, mostly because I assumed he wouldn't tell me. I'd been braced for his nice guy act to dry up at some point, either when I stopped providing dye-related helpful hints or if I asked too many nosy questions. So, I'd restrained myself mightily.

Donovan shrugged, his eyes still tracking Colette Cray as she made her way up and down the beach. "I don't know. I think they found it in her car? The evidence must implicate her, or they wouldn't have made the arrest."

Don't get me wrong, my teenage self would have voted Jeena Harding as 'girl mostly likely to grow up to murder some skank for sleeping with her husband' without the slightest hesitation. But I couldn't quite picture it now. Not least because I couldn't imagine her setting foot in a laundry shed, or using her own washing machine.

Honestly, a white dress. I wouldn't go near a bath of dye while wearing white. Wearing twelve men's shirts wouldn't be enough to protect a dress like that. The dye had soaked all the way through the fibres. It would have stained what was underneath.

(It would have stained the wrist or the arm. Perhaps it did. Perhaps that was how they knew to arrest her.)

"There's more," Donovan went on.

Colette turned at that point, and waved at him.

He stood up, every inch the serious security professional, and nodded. She started heading up towards the sand, bouncing in our general direction.

I had to be quick if I wanted to get more out of him. "More than your sister-in-law being arrested for her late husband's fashion-designing BFF and/or girlfriend?" And/or business partner in the Chameleon brand...

"They've opened Ethan's hit-and-run case again," Donovan said heavily. "At least, they're back investigating it actively, not sure if it was ever closed. They've impounded Jeena's car."

"Because of Meegan's video?" In which she cast suspicion on the entire Brady family... Oh, hell. Had Jeena killed them both?

What kind of frock would you wear to run your husband off the road in a fatal accident?

"Something like that." Donovan shrugged heavily. "I never really thought — Dad and Ethan have always gone running on country roads. I told them it was stupid dangerous, there's a treadmill at the house." He motioned vaguely at Colette Cray with a bitter twist of his mouth. "But some people don't like to make things easy for themselves. Dad and Ethan laughed it off. When I first heard about Ethan's accident — well, I'd been telling him for years that could happen. I was angry about it, but I didn't think…"

As Colette Cray charged towards us, flashing a million dollar smile, a flock of teens in vigil-green scarves finally recognised her. They squealed and swooped in, holding their phones out from a mostly respectful distance. She smiled and laughed with them, agreeing to selfies.

Donovan, on high alert, started moving in that direction.

"What didn't you think?" I called after him.

He glanced over his shoulder, his mind clearly on his client rather than me. "I didn't think anyone would do that deliberately," he said. "Not to Ethan, no one hated him that much. Even Jeena. She could just divorce him and take all his money. But Ethan and my dad are a similar height and build, they both wear the same kinds of tracksuit. If someone meant to hit him, to knock him off the road, well… maybe it wasn't Ethan they were trying to hurt."

"Are we still talking about Jeena?" Was she more likely to try to kill her overbearing father-in-law, or her cheating, dress-designing husband?

Donovan's face clouded over. "If you're talking people who want to kill my father, it wouldn't be a short list," he growled.

"We're going to need a chart," announced Paisley, when I returned from the juice bar with a smoothie for each of us, since I still had five minutes left of my break.

"You sound like Trace."

"Trace is a good organiser. I appreciate that in a person."

I huffed at them. "The police have arrested Jeena for killing Meegan, and it sounds like they're trying to get her for Ethan too. Why would that require a chart?"

Paisley waggled their eyebrows at me over the top of the smoothie. "Sorry, are we trusting the police to always arrest the right people, now? That's not exactly your brand."

I had a lot of feelings about the fact that something I said to Inspector Rosenthal yesterday might have got a woman arrested who was... okay, not a friend. Never a friend. But a person I was at school with. That meant something, didn't it?

Apparently, I wouldn't wish wrongful arrest on my worst enemy. Good to know.

Paisley was way ahead of me, drawing up columns on a whiteboard. Why did everyone I know own whiteboards? Where were they all coming from? "Okay, so we need two motive columns, for Ethan's death and for Meegan's. Then we'll look at means, and opportunity."

"Three columns," I told her, giving in to the inevitable. At least the shop was quiet. Mostly because all the local teenagers had bought out every green item we had, and their intense clusters around the shop (not to mention the growing heap of floral wreaths and candles out the front) were making other potential customers uncomfortable. Also, it was the middle of the week, which was always slow.

"Has there been another murder I don't know about?" Paisley frowned.

I rolled my eyes, and snatched the marker. "Donovan told me that Ethan and their dad were of a similar build, dressed the same, both jogged on country roads at night. So Ethan's death could have been motivated by someone wanting to kill Gavin. And from what Donovan says, that's a long list."

"Okay," said Paisley. "Put Donovan in the Ethan column, but not the Gavin column. If he killed his brother while trying to kill his dad, there's no way he would have told you that, right? That would be a really stupid double bluff."

"I don't think Donovan was even in Tasmania when his brother died."

"We're looking at Motive! Means and Opportunity go on entirely different whiteboards." More eyebrow waggling from Paisley. "If only there was some way you could check that information about Donovan's where-abouts, b-t-dubs."

They weren't wrong. Inspector Rosenthal had given me his mobile number in case I had any further informa-tion. That could go both ways, couldn't it? And what better way to test that out than when we weren't the same room?

On impulse, I rang the number.

"Rosenthal," he answered in a clipped voice.

"Hi, uh. This is Samantha Sullivan. Remember how I provided some key information for your case recently, as an expert witness? It was green, and laundry-related."

His sigh was well and truly long-suffering. "I remember."

"I was wondering if you could confirm for me whether

Donovan Brady was out of the state when Ethan Brady was killed."

"Why would you need to know that?" He sounded suspicious, and rightly so.

"I'm thinking about dating him and I want to make extra sure that he's not a murder suspect," I said quickly.

Paisley hid a snort up their sleeve.

Another long-suffering sigh, but Rosenthal clearly felt like he still owed me one. At least one. "Donovan Brady flew into Hobart Airport the day after he received the news of his brother's death. I believe he already had a ticket to come here for work reasons, but exchanged it for an earlier flight. That's all in order. We do not consider him a person of interest at this time."

"Thanks."

"His alibi for Meegan Kelly's death checks out too."

"Wait, what?" Unsolicited information. Huh. "I mean, I mostly am his alibi, right?"

"Our forensics people were so excited about an opportunity to test how long it takes for dye to soak into hair and skin that they got a report in faster than usual. They believe Ms Kelly was in the water for at least two hours when they got their hands on her, which suggests it was at least an hour before you discovered the body. Given that her Instagram video was released at 5:05, that narrows the window for her murder to between that and around 6:30 in the evening."

Trace and I had already done the timeline for that one. 6:30 was around the time Donovan ditched me in West Hobart with his dad, which was at least a twenty minute drive. So her theory of he and his dad doing away with

Meegan as a joint project was well out. Not that I'd been overly convinced by it.

"So, I'm *completely* his alibi."

"Yes, you are. I hope that sets your mind at ease."

"Inspector, are you overly invested in my love life at this point?"

"Just trying to be helpful. Uh, speaking of which."

Not an ominous segue at all. "Yes?"

"Your sister asked me out to dinner," he said, in a calm and measured tone as if he was asking the time. "It occurred to me that you might be uncomfortable with that, given our history."

Oh, Trace. Bloody hell. Somehow, I managed to reply politely, since it wasn't in my best interest to inform him I was going to strangle my sister. "That's very considerate of you. But it's fine. I hope you have a nice time."

After I hung up, I banged my head gently on the counter.

Paisley was dealing with a customer, an older woman looking for a grandma of the bride outfit that 'didn't look frumpy'. After a good chat and a few wild suggestions, Paisley sent her off with a glittery jacket and repurposed designer slip dress that fit her figure excellently.

"That was the first customer in two hours who didn't want to buy something green," Paisley noted as the grandma left. "Would it be bad if we threw together a dye batch of all our old stock that's hard to shift?"

"I don't know about bad," I said. "But I think blending green dye at this point would give me a panic attack. Also, we're still not allowed to use the laundry shed."

"Ugh, that sucks. We're going to need those washing machines back!"

I should have asked Rosenthal for that on the phone instead of being so nice about the fact that he wanted to date my sister.

"The good news is we can take Donovan off all the columns," I reported. "He's in the clear, alibi-wise."

"Well, fine," Paisley grumbled. "But I'm putting Gazza Brady in all the columns. Except his own, I suppose he wouldn't try to murder himself. And if he did murder his son while mistaking him for himself, well. That's a special level of incompetence."

"Did Gavin even know Meegan?"

"Maybe he blamed her for turning his son on to fashion design! From what Leon and Harper were saying, he's all bent out of shape about it now he's found out, but what if he knew all along?"

I frowned at the chart. "Okay, but what's Gavin's motivation for running his son off the road?"

"He *really* hated fashion design…"

"You're both wrong."

We turned around quickly to see Morgaine standing in the doorway.

"We were working," I assured her, not sounding at all convincing.

"I've come up with a plan to dye everything green and sell it to the teen mourners," said Paisley brightly.

"No worries, it's a weird week and there are no customers." Morgaine came over to look at the chart. "What's Jeena's motive supposed to be?"

"Ethan and Meegan were having an affair," Paisley

told her. "Allegedly. Anyway, she thought they were."

They glanced at me and mouthed 'they totally were' in my direction.

Morgaine scoffed. "An affair. Do people really murder each other over that sort of thing these days?"

"It's a classic," Paisley said. "Evergreen murder motive."

Morgaine shook her head. "What you have here is a very wealthy young couple with no children. Why would Jeena commit two murders instead of just divorcing her husband, taking her share of the money, and then never having to see him again?"

Hmm. That was a good point. I'd thought something similar, when I first heard about Jeena's arrest.

My impression of current Jeena — widowed, 30-something, furious-at-the-world Jeena — was that she didn't clean her own home, or cater her own events. She'd even hired someone to take away the frocks, instead of stuffing them in garbage bags and setting them on fire. Would she really murder two people personally, rather than outsource the job to an expert?

I had a fleeting thought of Jeena contacting the local employment centre to hire an assassin. But no, Meegan's murder had been messy. An amateur job. And it was hard to imagine a professional hit-man could make a decent living in Tasmania. Surely you'd have to go to the mainland for that.

Morgaine waved her hand at the chart. "This list of yours is all about feelings. You need to be considering money. Murder is a desperate act, and there's nothing makes people more desperate than money."

I thought about the Swoosh Hutch, and Leon looking so gutted about losing everything they'd built because Gavin Brady decided to take his frustrations out on them. Leon, with a bright green tattoo on his wrist… who had come up with the idea of Chameleon in the first place, perhaps? Certainly, had designed the lizard logo that was stamped on the drawings.

If Ethan was willing to steal a business idea and a logo from someone he shared a studio with, what else might he have done? And who might have wanted him dead?

"Paisley, I think we're going to need another chart."

I'D FORGOTTEN ABOUT THE MONEY. NOT JUST THE RISING
wealth of the Brady family, with their gleaming glass
house and their electric car empire. But the $10,000 paid to
Ethan Brady by *Impeccable Magazine*, for the rights to the
photo shoot for a mysterious collection. And the $50,000
paid to him for Colette Cray's wedding dress.

Where had all that money gone?

I suppose it all depended, really, whether Ethan and/or
Meegan were the designer known as Chameleon. If either
of them had that money, they certainly hadn't poured it
into the Swoosh Hutch, not if there were still unpaid bills
Meegan had been hiding from her studio partners.

I was itching to call Inspector Rosenthal with more
questions, mostly about whether the police had looked into
the financial records of both victims. Would it be wrong to
beg Trace to slip him a few sneaky murder questions on
their forthcoming date?

Then there was Leon (Chame*leon?*) and Harper. I
wrote their names on the whiteboard and frowned. If they

were involved, they hadn't seen any of the profit. Unless Leon lied to me.

Paisley sat up very straight suddenly, eyes on their phone. "Um. *Um.*"

"What?"

"There's a livestream on Colette Cray's website right now that we need to watch. According to Twitter, she found her wedding dress."

"Thank goodness for that," said Morgaine. "That should reduce the drama around here."

"Not so's you'd notice," said Paisley, tapping away on the shop laptop. They rotated the screen so we could all watch the livestream.

A couple of glammed-up teenage girls in green armbands sidled into the shop. "Excuse me, can charge our... OMG they're watching it!"

"Watching what?" I asked, but everyone shushed me. The teens clustered around the laptop with us.

The video showed Colette, a pleasantly symmetrical 20-something with artfully rumpled dark hair, dressed 'down' in a hoodie and natural makeup. She was filming herself, selfie-style, as she headed down a suburban street that looked familiar to me. As she walked, you could see passers by turning to give her weird looks, probably because she was filming herself rather than because she was famous.

"... not going to tell you, because it's still secret," she said, eyes dancing behind perfect mascara. "I love you all, but if we leak the wedding date and location that means there will be helicopters and paps, and it will turn into this whole thing. Boring! But as promised I do have an amazing reveal just for you, right now. Today, we're going to meet the designer of my wedding dress. Live on camera, I'm going to introduce you to the one and only... Chameleon!"

"What," I said out loud.

The two teenagers squeed to each other and crept closer to the laptop.

"I hope she's not heading to a cemetery or a police morgue," remarked Paisley. "Because this could get dark very quickly."

"I don't like this," said Morgaine in an ominous voice. That surprised me. Up until now, she had been the least engaged in any of this murder and wedding dress nonsense — remaining above the drama with her casual, practical advice. But Morgaine now stared at the laptop like it was about to burst into flames.

Colette continued to walk along, chatting away. She turned a corner and I suddenly realised what street she was on.

"Hang on, that's..."

"Yep," said Morgaine.

Now I understood her face of doom. She knew what was coming, and it wasn't going to be pretty.

Colette Cray stopped in front of a boutique I knew well. She framed it at first so you could only see the wedding dresses in the front window, then tilted it up to show the Bridezillion sign.

"Can you believe it? My dress is right in there. And here's the designer — she's been anonymous since her first killer look hit Instagram last year, but now she's come out of the shadows. Meet Vivi Wave: Chameleon!"

Vivi, Morgaine's sister, popped out of her front door, blonde and shiny, wearing a silver jumpsuit with pockets all the way down to the ankles. Her makeup was professionally done, so she was clearly prepared for this moment.

Vivi held a hot pink garment bag, fully zipped up. "Hi, Colette! Hi, Colette's fans. I'm really excited to meet you all and talk about the magical fairy tale dress I've designed for the wedding of the year. We call it the Titania, and it was inspired by a certain hit Shakespearean movie."

"I got to wear some amazing outfits in that!" Colette giggled.

The two of them chatted a little about *A Midsummer Night's Dream* (coming to DVD and streaming soon) and Colette's chosen wedding theme ("fairy sparkle everywhere, I'm so inspired!") before they waved their goodbyes, promising another vid soon. The Bridezillion logo was flashed one last time before the livestream shut off.

"OMG, where is that shop?" demanded one of the teenagers, like her life depended on it.

"Sandy Bay," I told her, and rattled off the address.

The two of them bolted, holding their dead phones like they were trying to will them back to life.

"I mean," said Paisley faintly. "I guess if everyone thinks Meegan wasn't Chameleon after all, they'll stop holding vigils outside our shop? Yay for the win?"

"But Vivi's *not*, right?" I said. "She can't be. I went to her shop with Donovan earlier in the week, I swear that was the first time she saw the sketch of the Titania. She was really excited, she even…" I paused, remembering how Vivi had darted away, holding Donovan's phone.

Long enough to take a few screen caps of the design, maybe? "Has she *stolen* Chameleon's identity? I know she had an opportunity to pinch the design. She must have sewn like the wind to get it made up in time."

Someone stole the Chameleon identity. Could Leon have been referring to Vivi, not Ethan?

"We can't prove she's not Chameleon," said Paisley. "Can we? We don't know who they are either. We guessed Chameleon might have been Ethan or Meegan, or Ethan *and* Meegan, but we can't prove any of it."

"I'm going to kill her," said Morgaine quietly, getting to her feet. "What the hell is she trying to get away with? What's the point?"

"Fifty thousand dollars," Paisley coughed.

"Colette Cray already paid for the dress," I reminded them. "She wouldn't pay more now, surely?"

"Vivi's getting plenty of publicity for her shop," said Morgaine. It was always a worry when she got still and quiet.

Paisley skimmed through their phone. "No Insta updates from Chameleon, endorsing the vid on Colette's site. So Vivi doesn't have access to the account. If she did, she'd have put something up straight away to support her claim. Is it illegal to pretend to be someone who's anonymous and also maybe dead?"

"I mean," I hesitated. "If Vivi really isn't Chameleon, saying she is would be fraud, right?" I felt guilty even suggesting that. "Not that the police would probably care to put a fraud case together unless she received money under false pretences."

"This is worse than money," said Morgaine. "Colette

Cray has millions of fans. If this all comes out and Vivi is exposed for lying, she'll be obliterated. And it won't just be her shop that gets targeted. Fashionably Late is already tied to Meegan Kelly's death. Vivi's my sister. Will anyone believe we weren't in on it?"

We all went quiet for a moment, thinking about the consequences of today's dramatic announcement.

"Maybe Vivi actually was Chameleon all along?" I ventured.

Morgaine gave me the mother of withering looks. "Do you really think that, Sam?"

I'd been trying to put these pieces together for so long, I barely even had to consider the possibility. "No. It's not her. No way."

"Try telling that to the internet," said Paisley, already knee-deep in the comments. "A pop star said it, so it must be true. #visiblechameleon is trending."

Three hours after we watched the livestream announcing to the world that Vivi Wave of Bridezillion was the mysterious designer Chameleon, we got a visit from Colette Cray herself. Donovan Brady was the first through the door, in his usual suit and giant sunglasses, looking completely 'on the clock' as a bodyguard.

Two more security people took up a stance in front of our window, partially blocking the light into the shop.

Then Colette entered, all celeb glamour, ready to be photographed from any candid angle in a tiny sundress bright with yellow daisies.

Behind her, Vivi Wave in that stupid silver jumpsuit of hers, cradling the hot pink garment bag and looking smug. The only mitigating factor here was that no one was trying to film anyone else, though I was pretty sure Paisley was tempted.

Morgaine stood up, politely warm. You'd never know what she was thinking if you hadn't heard her ranting over tea and biscuits a few minutes ago. "Can we help you?"

Colette's face broke into a completely gorgeous, natural smile. Clearly one of those celebs with actual people skills. Being nice to 'ordinary folk' while famous is a specialised skill, and it can get an attractive person very far indeed.

"Sorry for the interruption!" she gushed. "I know it's been a crazy few days for your shop."

That was one way of putting it.

"Addie Chambers from *Impeccable*… you know Addie."

"I know Addie," Morgaine agreed. All her attention was on Colette, completely shutting out her sister. Brutal.

"She wants to do the super secret Titania shoot in three days, now we have the dress safe and secure!" Colette gave a dazzling smile to Donovan, though I don't think I was imagining a slight edge to that one. Nothing like losing a $50,000 dress for a week to make you lose confidence in your security guard. "She showed me a bunch of stills from the previous shoot, and they are am-ahhh-zing. I want my gown to have the Fashionably Late touch too, to tie it all together."

"We were hoping to borrow one of your veils from the

photo shoot," Vivi said helpfully. "Something borrowed, something green. You know how it is."

I had a flash memory of that last, torn green veil clinging to the Hills Hoist, just before I found Meegan's body. I shivered.

"Oh, I don't just want a veil," said Colette, clapping her hands. "Are you kidding? I mean yes, those veils were gorge, with all the silk flowers and ripped gauze, I totally want one. But after seeing how the collection was staged, there's no way I'm going to be stuck in a boring old white dress like I'm *anybody*. I want the Fashionably Late magic."

Vivi's smug smile faltered. "Sorry? I thought you liked the Titania."

"Oh, I adore it," Colette gushed. "It's a spectacular dress, even better than I thought when I first saw the sketches. But it's not quite perfect yet, not compared to what it could be." Her eyes fell on me, and a hungry expression took over her face. "You're Samantha Sullivan, aren't you?"

Startled at being addressed directly by a celebrity (honestly, she was so beautiful it was like staring into the *sun*), I nodded. "That's right," I managed to say.

"Well, then. I hear you're the one to talk to about dyeing my wedding dress green!"

People think of fashion as being all about the modern, the new, the fresh. Moving forward. Even an upcycled clothes boutique like Fashionably Late taps into what people want to wear *now*, whether it's a brand new pair of painted silk culottes, or a renovated minidress from 1966.

But fashion as a concept has been with us for a very long time, and often when people think they're doing something original, they're actually following a tradition that goes back hundreds of years.

Cuts and styles of clothes, sure. Most people recognise that if you're wearing flared trousers or platform shoes in the 21st century, it's the return of a retro favourite. Ditto the revival of fringed gowns and headbands earlier this decade, or the inexplicable eternal popularity of the corset. Doc Martens. Blundstone Boots. Even the bubble skirt made a comeback not long ago, and no one saw that coming.

Colours follow fashions, too. Try buying pastels in a season when all the shops are selling brights, or a teal jacket when everything is monochrome. Sometimes colour trends are driven by emotion, or celebrity, or a brand new technique. Purple is associated with royalty because the Ancient Romans thought it was fancy way back when, and it was an expensive process involving the torturing of whelks (just to add that extra *je ne sais quois*). No one felt the need to buy a new white dress for their wedding until Queen Victoria made the look popular. Have you heard of Millennial Pink, or Gen Z Yellow? There was a time when pink was reserved for boy babies, because it was the softer version of the Extremely Manly colour of red. Now, apparently, pink belongs to the Millennials, a generational tag that makes less and less sense as they (okay, *we*) march towards middle age.

And then, there's green. A tricky colour, green. Not

counting St Patrick's Day, it's been associated with bad luck and sinister superstition for a long time, especially in clothes, for one simple reason: green used to kill people.

In the 19th century, a particular bright emerald hue was created from arsenic, and it's not an exaggeration to say it went viral.

Bright green gowns and gloves and hair ornaments were the fashionable must-haves for season after season. Then people started getting ill and dropping dead… the factory workers who worked with the fabric, and in some rare cases, the fashionable ladies who wore the clothes. A green head-dress contained enough arsenic to kill twenty people, while one of the ballgowns might hold enough to murder over a hundred and fifty.

What is most extraordinary is that everyone knew the dresses were dangerous. Experts investigated, and their findings proved that the green fabric caused illness, skin damage and death. Newspapers ran cartoons of skeletons dancing in ballgowns. It was a public health crisis and a joke at the same time — probably because it was a public health crisis affecting mostly women, so of course it was 'ridiculous'.

The fashion took decades to die out, even after the scientific findings had been published.

The truth was, the nineteenth century was full of poison — in the curtains, in the paint, in the wallpaper, as well as the clothes. Some people kicked up a stink about it, but no one managed to stamp it out. Female activists tried to put an end to the toxic frocks, but poison green was just so pretty. It could not be stopped.

And of course, the majority of the deaths were not the

women wearing the clothes at all, but the poor, badly-paid women who made them in the first place…

There's a reason that fashion houses still claim that 'seamstresses don't like green' and it has nothing to do with superstition.

Meegan Kelly wasn't murdered by the dye in the bath where she died, but I was now always going to associate that particular shade of green with finding her dead body. When I closed my eyes I could still see her pale hair, floating on the surface. Her purple tips went muddy, but her whitened hair took the colour beautifully.

I loved dyeing fabrics. I didn't want to lose that love, not after I'd worked so hard to build my new skillset. It was the first thing I got good at, in this new life of mine. But it was a long while before I'd feel ready to dye anything else green.

Colette Cray was not a patient person. You could tell by looking at her that she expected to get her own way. She was a pop star, after all. Celebrity meant she was used to everyone jumping in the air the second she suggested it might look cute.

Vivi looked horrified, so at least this wasn't part of her plan. Of course she wouldn't want me stealing her thunder. It was the first time I considered that she might be the designer of the Titania after all. How would it feel to toil over a gorgeous, career-making wedding gown, only for it to be handed straight over to some amateur with a bath full of dye?

Morgaine had an odd look on her face that I took to mean 'trying not to laugh.'

Paisley actually did burst out into a bark of laughter and then looked embarrassed.

"Well?" said Colette, daring me to object. "I want a green wedding dress, and I hear you're the one to make it happen. Let's get messy."

16

THE MOST IMPORTANT THING ABOUT COLETTE CRAY'S wedding gown, apart from the fact it had been missing for several days and I was convinced the person claiming to have made it was lying, was that it had to stay a secret.

Secrecy around The Dress was standard for weddings, regardless of celebrity status. But of course, not every bride had half the paparazzi in the country (and a whole generation of teens on social media) hungry for a sneak peek of what she might be wearing.

After Colette Cray bulldozed her way into Fashionably Late, Morgaine talked her into showing me the wedding dress in private, as her 'dye consultant,' keeping everyone else away. Vivi protested, of course, but Morgaine distracted her with some general sisterly shade, giving me and Colette an escape route into the studio room at the back of the shop.

Just me and a famous person, la-la-la.

"So," Colette said, unzipping the garment bag with flourish. "What do you think?"

Here's the thing: it was a great dress.

Speaking as someone who has seen so many variations on the humble wedding dress that they pretty much form a haze of static behind my eyelids… yeah, this was a nice one. Big bell-shaped skirt, reasonably frothy, plenty of layers but not too much meringue. Cut short, to defy expectations.

(Chameleon liked their brides to show a healthy amount of calf.)

Well-tailored bodice, wide straps. A flattering neckline. A gauze cape hanging down the back, shaped like fairy wings. It ticked all the boxes of a solid 9 out of 10.

It was lovely. But… honestly, it was more basic than I had expected from the sketch, and from the boldness of the other gowns.

If you hung this one in the middle of the Chameleon collection, I don't think I'd even pick it for my top five. And I'm not only saying that because it was white. The other dresses had breathed — there was a confidence in their seams, in the tailoring. A breathtaking arrogance, combined with expert stitching.

From the sketch I'd seen, however briefly, on Donovan's phone, I'd imagined something far more dramatic from the fairy wing cape. Real hand-made lace, perhaps? This one was pretty but simple, without even the veins of the wings machine stitched into the soft, floaty fabric. Someone had cut corners to save time.

It was a nice dress, but it wasn't amazing. And while the core design was spectacular, it only took a quick look at the under-seams to convince me that the person who put it together it had not been involved in the rest of the Chameleon collection at all.

"Well?" said Colette impatiently, bouncing on her heels. "I want it to look at least as amazing as the others. It needs green right?"

"Oh yes," I assured her. "It needs green."

By the time Colette Cray swept Vivi and Donovan off on the next stop of her celebrity tour of Tasmania, we had come up with a plan. I convinced her that she didn't want the dresses to look exactly like the others, and she was amenable to a compromise that would help tie the Titania to the rest of the collection while still looking like a special snowflake.

I suggested a net of green silk cobwebs and flowers, to drape over the bodice and the top of the skirt in a final layer, adding that wispy magic I remembered from the sketch. (Those odd round shapes from the original design could be reflected in that net — whoever made this dress had left them out, probably because they had no idea why they were included in the first place.)

I didn't mention this part to Colette, but I was pretty sure we could improve on the wings, too — make them a little more obvious, add some texture.

We also discussed dyeing a couple of the under layers of the frothy skirt deep purple, so it would show as a flash of colour underneath the white. Too late, after I talked her into it I realise that the reason such a colour combination had been on my mind was because of the late Meegan Kelly and her purple-dipped white hair. Oh, well. Hopefully no one else would make that connection.

"You're a wonder!" Colette said, leaving the dress behind as she waved and retreated. "I leave it all in your capable hands! Smooches!"

Vivi gave me a death glare as she left. Donovan acted like he had never met me before in his life.

"Um," Paisley said, turning to look at Morgaine. "Is the shop insured well enough to cover a $50,000 dress being left here overnight?"

"Good point," said Morgaine. "Bring it with us to the pub."

"I wouldn't worry," I told them. "That isn't the Titania."

They stared at me.

"Okay," said Morgaine finally. "Bottle shop, not pub. This conversation should *not* happen in public."

It wasn't technically an intervention, but with Trace, Paisley and Morgaine all sitting around Aunt Harriet's kitchen table and staring at me, it sure felt like one. Our collection of whiteboard charts was getting out of hand.

Daisy was in her room, quietly building a life model of the digestive tract out of old toilet rolls. I was kind of jealous.

It was raining outside, glorious Hobart weather for the middle of spring. We only had another month or so of rain being an annoyance instead of something to be grateful for in between bushfire warnings.

Trace pulled out a bottle of wine, which happened to be Bottle #1 of the sparkling white I'd stocked up on to celebrate her divorce papers. She filled champagne flutes for everyone with the confidence of a woman who knew there was a second bottle in the fridge.

Morgaine had brought a six pack of local cider to supplement the sparkling white. Paisley, who had been of legal drinking age for less than a year, produced the mixings for rum and coke, but grudgingly accepted the sparkling white instead.

"I'm not accusing my sister of faking a whole dress to pretend to be Chameleon," said Morgaine, to start us all off. "But please tell me how you know the dress is definitely a fake."

"The stitching style," I said immediately. "The materials, the stitch choices, even the thread... they were all inconsistent with the Chameleon dresses I handled. This dress is perfectly fine, but the others were amazing."

"Perhaps this one was rushed." Ah, a devil's advocate argument. I could tell that Morgaine agreed with me. She'd seen the dresses too, even if she hadn't spent quite so much time up close and personal with them.

"Oh, I'm *sure* Chameleon took their time over the entire collection but did a last minute rush job on the celebrity showcase piece." I rolled my eyes. "Yes, it was rushed. Clearly it was rushed. And it shouldn't have been."

Morgaine nodded slowly.

"Designers don't always make their own dresses," Paisley mused. "There's nothing to say that Chameleon made the original collection. Maybe Vivi hired a better dressmaker to construct her designs, and had to replace this one after it went missing, so did it herself — or got someone not as good this time around."

"Sure," said Trace. "But you all think Vivi is lying, right?"

Paisley and I glanced uncomfortably at Morgaine.

"Believe me," she sighed. "None of this is a shock. There's a reason Diana won't have Vivi working in the family business."

"You saw the original sketch, right?" Paisley pressed me.

"Sure," I said. "This dress is based on that design, but… if it was made at the same time as the others, I will eat a dozen green wedding veils." I had been thinking through the potential timeline all day. "I'm sure Vivi saw the sketch for the first time when Donovan showed it to her last week. She had enough time alone with his phone to send herself a screencap, or to photograph the screen from her own phone. She threw together her version to grab the credit."

"So the real Titania dress is out there somewhere!" Trace said triumphantly.

I hesitated. "Probably. But um. Do we do anything about this? Colette Cray seems reasonably happy with her dress, once we've added the dyed elements. What would be the benefit of exposing Vivi?"

Morgaine nodded glumly. "It would cause drama. A lot of drama. And whether it was us or someone else who exposed her, Fashionably Late would still be tainted by association."

"But it's not fair," said Paisley. "She's not claiming to be Chameleon for this one occasion, she has to keep it going. She's gonna steal their reputation."

"And if the real Chameleon was still alive," I said heavily. "They'd be able to contradict her."

"It's awfully convenient for her," said Trace, already down to the bones of her first glass of sparkles. "Chameleon is too dead to defend their identity. How do we know Vivi isn't behind that, too?"

Slightly shocked, we all sat with that possibility for a second.

"I do not think my sister is a murderer," Morgaine said firmly. "She is an ethical black hole with an eye for opportunity, but I don't think she would have drowned another person in my bathtub."

"No, that would require getting her hands dirty," Paisley snarked. They didn't have a lot of time for Vivi either.

"Wait," said Trace. "I thought there was an arrest already. I was waiting for you to share the gossip," she added to me. "Catch us up!"

That reminded me that I had known about her upcoming date all day and hadn't teased her about it once. "Oh, didn't your boyfriend tell you?"

"Inspector Rosenthal is very professional, actually," she said snippily. Then, softer: "You don't mind about that, do you, Sam?"

My feelings about it were complicated, so very complicated. I was starting to think that Rosenthal was a decent person, but I still wanted to run away whenever I saw him. I also didn't want to unpack all those feelings in front of witnesses. "I'll get over it. You've dated worse."

"I married worse." She looked so grateful for my understanding. Oh hell. Did she have more than one date in mind with this bloke?

"That goes without saying." I never resist the opportunity to trash talk her ex.

"So?" Trace added impatiently. "I've been dying all day. Who was arrested?"

"Jeena Harding-Brady, according to her brother-in-law," I said heavily. "Same problem with Vivi — do we really think she would hold someone under water in a bathful of dye? Even less believable, she'd have to have done it while wearing a white dress."

"Oh, I remember her from school!" Trace exclaimed. "Yeah, I see what you mean, she's more of a stab you in the back sort of girl."

"Poison your martini," I agreed.

"Strangle you with a designer handbag."

"Anyway!" said Morgaine. "The point is, can we let this thing with Vivi run wild, or will it stuff up the whole investigation?"

"That's a good question," I said as the doorbell rang. "I'm going to get that so I don't have to think of an answer yet."

I wasn't expecting anyone in particular. But I'll tell you what I really wasn't expecting as I peered out into the rain: a damp, bedraggled Jeena Harding-Brady, makeup-free and wearing a soggy lime green suit.

"Are you lost?" I asked in my surprise. I couldn't imagine she had come here of her own volition.

Jeena looked miserable, but still had enough poise to roll her eyes and summon her last vestige of snark. "Don't even pretend you're not playing amateur detective, Samantha Sullivan. I need your help, and I'm *not* going to ask twice."

You could never accuse her of hiding how she felt. "Fair enough," I said, and opened the door wide. "Luckily for you, we have wine."

17

JEENA LOOKED ABOUT AS UNCOMFORTABLE SURROUNDED
by Aunt Harriet's quilty clutter as I might have expected. It
was the opposite of her magazine spread life aesthetic. By
the time we reached the cozy, crowded kitchen, she looked
like a cat with all her hackles raised. "I might have known
there was a gang of you," she sneered.

There was a time in my life when her disapproval
meant social death and personal devastation, but I'd taken
a lot of knocks since then, and Jeena Harding-Brady had
little power to wither me. "Be nice or you don't get wine,"
I told her. I grabbed another champagne flute down from
the cupboard anyway, because she looked like she'd had a
pretty terrible day.

I introduced the others — Jeena didn't bat an eyelid at
Paisley's they/them pronouns which was the bare
minimum of human decency but still good to know — and
offered her the last chair. "You said you wanted my help."

I was both petty and practical enough to make her
confirm it in detail.

"You know I do," said Jeena between gritted teeth. She accepted the glass of bubbles that I passed her. "I was taken in for questioning this morning. I've been in police custody for most of the day." She sounded slightly disassociated, like she was in shock. I didn't blame her. I'd been there.

Well, not quite there. Donovan had said 'arrested.' Surely he knew the difference.

"We knew that," said Paisley helpfully.

Jeena looked distracted. "Is it in the media already?" she murmured.

"I mean, probably," said Paisley.

We hadn't thought to check.

"I'd stay off Facebook," Morgaine advised.

Jeena drained half of her glass in a couple of savage swallows. "I can't believe this. They had some — *arse* in a plastic suit taking samples of my washing machine. And they think — they just kept asking questions. Thank goodness for my lawyer or I might still be in there."

Trace leaned in, vibrating with curiosity. "Do they think you killed both of them, or just the woman who was sleeping with your husband?"

"Trace," I snapped.

"What?"

"You can't ask her that!"

"But I want to know the answer."

The extremely personal question snapped Jeena out of her haze. She gave Trace a poisonous glare, looking much more herself. "I don't care whether or not he was sleeping with her," she said sharply. "He was making *those dresses* with her. That's worse."

She was shaking. For someone who said she didn't care if her husband had cheated on her, she sure looked betrayed.

"So, he *was* Chameleon!" Paisley crowed, giving Morgaine a high-five.

A thought that had been niggling at the back of my head since I first saw E.J.'s belongings spilling out of those cardboard box came sharply into focus. "I want to show you something," I told Jeena, and drew her out of the kitchen. "Give us a minute!" I called to the others, to keep them out of our hair.

They grumbled but stayed put.

"I really should be getting home," Jeena said stiffly, standing in the middle of Aunt Harriet's quilt-and-crochet layered wonderland like she was worried she might catch something from all these handicrafts. "This was a terrible mistake. I can't take any more of this. I thought you were going to help."

"I can't help until I have the whole picture. I think I'm starting to see it now. Check this out."

I had brought home a cardboard box from the Swoosh Hutch, stuffed with the most interesting finds from E.J.'s belongings. Thanks to Donovan abandoning me to go yell at his dad, I didn't feel even slightly guilty about it. Now I lifted out the top book and flipped it open to a familiar page. "See this outfit?"

It was a sketch of a jacket, nicely tailored, with a dramatically over-sized collar. The colour was bright red, very close to one of my favourite vermilion shades of dye, and the cuffs had a dapper triangular shape to them. The trousers matched, soft and wide. It looked glamorous and comfortable. It looked majestic.

Around the sketch were written a bunch of criticisms and pointy arrows. *Too boxy. Stupid colour. Lengthen the trousers. Weak lines.*

"See, what's interesting," I went on. "Is that it looks like the designer really hated this particular piece. And yet the outfit that a famous actress wore to the Scarlet Stiletto Awards is identical to this sketch. You can see pics online if you search. No detail was changed when they made it. And that made me think, maybe the handwriting and the drawings come from two different people."

We'd been thinking for some time that Chameleon represented a collaboration, but we'd assumed it was Ethan and Meegan. Now I had a different theory.

Jeena's mouth went very thin. "That's Ethan's handwriting," she admitted.

"That's what I thought. They're your drawings, though, aren't they?"

She looked at me, startled. "What?"

"I used to sit behind you in three classes at high school. It's a funny thing, sitting behind people. You get to know them without them even realising you are there. I know you, Jeena. I know you always told everyone how stupid art was, but you paid attention in that class, more than any other. And when you weren't sucking up to the art teacher, you were boasting to your friends about your gigs as a fashion model."

"I hardly even did that," Jeena said grouchily. "A couple of catalogue jobs, that was all."

"You never shut up about it at school."

"I liked, it, okay? Getting to pretend I was someone else for a few hours. It was fun."

"And you kept drawing clothes."

"It wasn't ever going to come to anything," she said sharply. "I wanted to apply design school, but my parents laughed. Get a receptionist job, they said. Earn some money. Then we'll see. So, I walked into the Brady car yard when they were advertising for a receptionist, and I never left. Married the boss's son. Changed my life."

I turned a few more pages of the sketchbook. This page was full of bubble dresses, a trend long out of fashion when we were at school. These were cute, with pastel shading over bold patterns. And of course, the style had made a recent comeback.

The words scribbled on this page were: *stupid, frivolous, why do you bother?* and *no one would wear this*.

Chameleon's mini-collection of peace silk bubble dresses caused an online sensation last summer. They were the reason that the Insta account had 1.2 million subscribers instead of like, four hundred. Those dresses made Chameleon a designer to watch.

Stupid. Frivolous. Why do you bother?

"It doesn't look like he was very supportive," I said calmly.

"Supportive," Jeena scoffed. "That's what he said when we first got together. Said he was trying to make me better. A real designer would listen to constructive criticism. Instead, he made me want to shove it all into a drawer and never look at it again."

I turned to another page of bubble dress designs that had the words *waste of space* scrawled over and over, the words overlapping the drawings as well as filling the white space. "So constructive."

"I wanted to make my own wedding dress," she said, starting to pace around the room. "Gavin, Ethan's dad. He was paying for everything, wouldn't even let my parents pay for the booze, and he got some prissy wedding planner, no offence, to make all the decisions. Nothing about that day was going to be mine. I wanted one thing that was special for me. The dress. On my special day. I can't sew — not really. But I knew I could draw something I liked and get a real dressmaker to make it up. He hated every idea I had, every sketch. I did over a dozen drawings and he hated every one of them. Said I'd look hopeless, that I was an amateur. Wasting my time. In the end I bought a damn dress off the rack with his credit card, to shut him up."

I thought of the giant blown-up wedding portraits in the foyer of their showcase home. "How did you feel about Gavin taking over your wedding?"

She scoffed. "Gavin doesn't care about any of it. He didn't care what happened on my wedding day as long as it was expensive and other people were impressed, and my family had no control over anything. I'm talking about Ethan, *Ethan* hated all my ideas."

Jeena was practically bouncing off the walls now, pacing erratically, her manicured fingers gripped tightly around the neck of the champagne flute. At least everything in this room was soft and padded. She wouldn't hurt herself on any sharp corners.

"I have that sketch book too," I said softly. I lifted it out. I'd been looking through them all, over the last few days when I had a spare moment. This was the book with drawing after drawing of the wedding collection, *the Chameleon collection*. The same designs Donovan had on his phone, though those were clean drawings without the commentary, and a cartoon lizard stamp added for authenticity.

(Leon's stamp, I was certain. And Leon's idea for a business name. Jeena's drawings. Ethan really had been a piece of work.)

These original drawings showed white dress after white dress, with notes scribbled by her husband. **Boring. Generic. Maybe if you lose a few kilos.**

"I gave up for years after that," said Jeena. "My parents were right, what was the point of going to design school? I'd been running the office at the car yard for years, I made good money, Ethan made *really* good money. Gavin let us live in his fancy house and drive his cars. I had a good life. No complaints."

She didn't sound like a woman with no complaints. She sounded like a woman who might have done something desperate to escape her own misery. No wonder Inspector Rosenthal thought she was guilty. No wonder he'd been questioning her all day.

She was guilty of something. Hiding something. But I still couldn't see that thing being murder.

If Jeena was anything like me, her pride would have meant she wasn't honest enough with the police to convince them of her innocence.

"So," I said. "When did you find out about Chameleon? When did you find out that Ethan and Meegan Kelly had were flogging off your designs on the mainland under their own label? That your work had been worn by celebrities?"

Jeena stood very still. Her face was composed back into that standard mean girl twist that meant she was about to say something vile, to lash out. I braced myself. "I don't know what you're talking about. I don't want to answer your questions any more."

"You came here for my help."

"How can you help me? Just because your life blew up in your face, Samantha Sullivan, doesn't mean you can go around — go around saying things —"

Wow, she was so miserable, she had actually run out of mean. I never thought I'd see the day.

"When did you find out about Chameleon, Jeena?"

"The day he died!" she burst out. "I walked in that room, his secret den, expecting video games and porn or some other stupid bloke stuff. Instead I found those dresses, *my dresses*, all hanging there, reminding me of what a shit my husband was. How long I put up with it. I let him make me small."

"You didn't kill Ethan." It wasn't a question. I'd never seriously thought that she had.

Jeena looked at me defiantly. "No."

"You didn't hit him with your car because you thought he was his dad? That was one of our working theories."

She gave me an odd look but said: "No," more quietly than before.

"What's the police evidence against you?"

Jeena took a deep breath and finally sat down, collapsing on a next of colourful crocheted throws with her champagne flute still clutched in one hand. The couch embraced her, like Aunt Harriet's ghost thought she needed a hug. Good luck climbing out of that comfy nest.

"That detective inspector, Rosenthal…"

"I'm familiar with his work."

"He thinks Ethan was hit by an electric car. Or at least, he thinks it's important that we as a family own a bunch of electric SUVs, because of how quietly they run. There's no obvious damage on any of the three cars, but they don't think he was hit that hard in the first place — he died from the fall over the barrier, it could have been caused by barely clipping him. If he didn't hear the car coming, he couldn't have got out of the way…" She stopped to swallow, like thinking about it all at once was overwhelming. "But we live in the country, none of our cars are pristine. Plenty of dings and scratches."

"That's theories," I said softly. "Not evidence." I had my own traumas around Inspector Rosenthal, but no one could say he arrested me without a clear line of evidence that he thought would take us all the way to trial. My ex-husband had managed to thoroughly implicate me in his fraud, making sure my name was everywhere in the records before he jumped ship to Bali.

I'd had a lot of time to think about that, afterwards. How lucky I was that the jury believed me, despite the clear evidence that I was up to my neck in Malcolm's crime. Even Rosenthal believed me, in the end. Evidence has a lot to answer for, but sometimes honest testimony can turn the tide.

"Evidence," Jeena said, nodding sharply. "I don't think they have any for Ethan's death. I can't think how they could. As for that girl…"

"Meegan."

"I only met her once, and I didn't like her. Even before I found out she'd been helping Ethan make those dresses, *my* dresses, and making themselves a fortune at my expense. I didn't kill her."

"The police think you did."

"Idiots," she scoffed. "I was wearing a white dress that day. I wouldn't go near a vat of green dye."

"That was the main reason I thought you didn't do it," I agreed.

"I know, right?" Jeena didn't seem offended that I was judging her practical fashion choices rather than good character. "Who would murder someone in the messiest way possible while wearing Prada?"

"Someone really stylish."

"Thank you," Jeena said, looking almost flattered. "No, wait. You're making fun of me."

"Tell me about the shirt."

"Ethan's shirt? I have no idea. It was found in my car, apparently, tucked into a corner of the boot. It had some green dye on it, and they reckon it was washed in my machine."

"They think you wore it to murder Meegan…"

Why hadn't they arrested her formally, if they had so much to go on?

"A pin-striped shirt, honestly, what protection is that? Maybe if it had been a full leather smock I might have risked the dress, but I don't own one. Besides, do they have any idea how much designer shirts cost? What a waste."

"Don't say any of this to a jury, it will not make you

look sympathetic. The police think you washed the shirt, failed to get the green dye out, and shoved it into a corner of your car."

"Exactly," said Jeena. "How stupid do they think I am? Now, if I was going to murder her…"

"Please stop planning better ways to murder the victim," I told her firmly. "It makes you look sociopathic."

"Better that than incompetent."

"No, not really."

Jeena paused, and drank the last mouthful of sparkling white from her glass. "Good point. I'll try to remember that. You are being more helpful than I expected."

"You came to me," I reminded her.

"Sure, because I was desperate and I thought you're pathetic enough that you wouldn't judge me."

Bless. "Are you sure it was Ethan's shirt? Don't he and his dad dress similarly? Same style, same size…" Same habit of jogging along country roads late at night.

"It was an Antony Diaz shirt, one of three that I bought Ethan for his last birthday. Gavin hates European designers, he says they're too flamboyant."

"Gavin sounds like such a peach." I sighed. "The best way to prove your innocence — the only way, really — is to figure out who actually did all this. Who wore the shirt, who washed the shirt, who *planted* the shirt in your car. Assuming that person killed Meegan, it would be helpful to know if they also killed your husband."

That was what saved me in the end, not my tears and abandoned wife act on the witness stand so much as the fact that my former personal assistant's sister came forward and admitted that my husband had been carrying on the affair for over a year, and her whole family knew I had nothing to do with it, because they'd been getting heaps of smug phone calls from Bali.

One witness. Phone records. And a smug couple who couldn't stop boasting how easily they'd got away with their crime.

Good old Lori. I sent her a Christmas card last year.

"Oh," said Jeena, lifting her chin slightly. I recognised the expression of a woman bracing herself to be humiliated. "I think I know who hit him with the car. And I can prove it wasn't me."

It's not often that I'm totally lost for words. "Why didn't you tell that to the police? Like, straight away? Why were those not the first words out of your mouth to them?"

"They barely asked about the night Ethan was hit. And I didn't want to explain it to anyone. Especially not —" she sighed, looking more human than I'd ever seen her. "I know people don't like me. But everything that happened the night Ethan died will make me look more guilty. It gives me more reason to have killed Meegan."

Motive was a bitch.

"Okay," I said more gently. "But if you have an alibi for Ethan's death, the police need to know. And if you're not the killer they are looking for, they need to know that too."

There was a cough from the kitchen door. Paisley leaned their head through, not even slightly apologetic. "Trace wants to know if we're calling her favourite Inspector right now, or if we're pouring out the hard stuff first."

I looked at Jeena. "That's up to you."

She stared at her empty glass, looking like the prisoner about to be led to the guillotine. "Both, please. I'll need at least one more drink. And a sandwich, if you have one. I don't think I should do this on an empty stomach."

"Trace," I called to the kitchen. "Get some nibbles out of the freezer. We're having company over!"

18

Before Trace's marriage fell apart, she was one of those business wives — you know, the kind who keeps a house shiny and perfect in case hubby has to bring home colleagues at the last minute, or suddenly host a party of twenty-four on a weekend. I'm pretty sure she pours most of those skills now into her new job as a real estate agent, advising clients on how to 'stage' their house so it looks amazing.

When Trace first moved in to this place, I half expected her to turn Aunt Harriet's cozy quilt nest into something more shiny and modern like her old life, but instead she let herself get comfortable, keeping it cluttered around the edges. Daisy definitely prefers living in a house that's not constantly folded into hospital corners. She's started leaving toys and drawings here and there, making the house feel like hers, instead of constantly tidying everything away into her room.

The one vestige remaining from Trace's old life is that when she's stressed, she makes hors d'oeuvres. Finger food, platter after platter. Meatballs, samosas, quiches and filled pastries. Spring rolls and chicken skewers, stuffed peppers and mushrooms. Blinis and risotto balls. She does this a lot when Daisy is at her dad's, stocking up the deep freeze when she makes too much for us to eat in one sitting.

I'd got used to it. There's always something to heat up in a hurry. Honestly, I've forgotten how to eat any other way.

This did mean that between us calling Inspector Rosenthal and him arriving with his sergeant in tow, we had turned Aunt Harriet's living room into an impromptu cocktail party. This was probably surprising to everyone who didn't actually live here.

To his credit, Inspector Rosenthal blinked once and then accepted a vegan sausage on a stick with a professional air.

Sergeant Deng (see, I'd learned his name!) took up a floral armchair closest to the mini cheese danishes, which showed he was a man with an eye for the strategic advantage.

"I hear you have more to share with us, Mrs Harding-Brady," the Inspector said his usual non-confrontational voice. I must be getting used to it — it didn't even stress me out any more.

Jeena, who had enough of a strategic mind that she had swapped out her champagne flute for a glass of orange juice shortly before the police arrived, looked remarkably composed. "Some details may have been left out in the interview room," she conceded.

To his credit, Inspector Rosenthal didn't suggest he

take her down to the station, clearly realising that this was a better environment for peeling back Jeena's layers of defence. Holding her in custody all day had done little, after all.

Also, her expensive shark of a lawyer wasn't here, which was a choice Jeena had made. I hoped she wouldn't come to regret it.

Rosenthal pulled out his trusty notebook. "Tell us about the night your husband died," he suggested. "Were you alone in the house?"

"It's our house, you know. Mine and Ethan's. Everyone thinks Gavin owns it, that he owns everything, but he put it in our names years ago. Our cars, too, though we're not allowed to change the bloody licence plates. We both have generous shares of the business. For tax reasons, I expect." Jeena blinked a few times. "It's mine, now. We had our wills done at the same time, so Ethan won't have had a chance to sign it all away to that grubby little sewing club-house and his so-called girlfriend."

There's a reason people always think the worst of Jeena when she opens her mouth.

"Gavin treats it as his house, though," she went on. "Turns up whenever he likes, eats food out of the fridge. He still has the master bedroom from when his wife was alive — Ethan never had the guts to ask for the room, so we made a second master suite, knocking two bedrooms together."

I was instantly curious about how Donovan fit into all this — had his father been as generous with him, given that he wasn't as involved in the family business and lived on the mainland?

"Was he at your house that night?" asked Inspector Rosenthal. "Gavin Brady?"

"Oh, yes. Watching that horrible show about under-cover drug dealers in the downstairs den all night. Even when Ethan and I had our fight, he didn't have the grace to leave and give us some space, oh no. He ordered pizza."

"So, you and Ethan had a fight," the Inspector contin-ued. He sounded like someone's friendly uncle, not a police officer at all. Very smooth.

"I'd found out," Jeena said calmly. "About the money. Sixty thousand dollars went into our account earlier this year, and went out again almost immediately. He thought I wouldn't notice if he spent it straight away, as if no one has ever looked at bank statements. I was checking things to send to the accountant, which Ethan was supposed to do last month, not that he ever does anything on time, and I found it."

"What did he spend the money on?" I asked.

Rosenthal gave me a warning look but let my question ride.

"A car," Jeena said with a hollow laugh. "Can you believe it? Electric, of course. From his father's yard, with all the usual discounts. He thought I'd never find out about it. But I have access to the business accounts, and I can put two and two together. I looked up the purchase. Very nice. Mint green Mini Cooper, straight off the factory floor. It's amazing he managed to keep it a secret this long."

"Not a birthday present for you, perhaps?" the Inspector remarked.

Jeena gave him a scornful look. "If you think men like Gavin and Ethan Brady bother to buy birthday presents for their wives, you haven't been paying attention. I don't think Cheryl ever had a birthday present from either of them back when she was around, she'd just order what she wanted and put it on Gavin's card. Donovan, of course, would send flowers to his mum to make up for the fact that he left home the second he could get away."

"You were angry about the car."

Jeena tilted her head, considering his words. "Angry about the money. Confused about the car. Mostly, I wanted to know where it all came from. Who was Impeccable Inc., and why had they paid my husband so much money?" She gave everyone a thin-lipped smile. "Of course, *Impeccable* couldn't mean the fashion magazine. I never considered that for a moment."

"Did he admit it?" I asked.

"Of course not. Gavin turned the TV up louder so he couldn't hear us fighting. Ethan went for a run, claiming he wasn't going to talk to me until I calmed down. As soon as he was gone, I went upstairs and broke open his private den. The room I was never allowed in."

"You found the wedding dresses," I breathed. This was where her story tied in to what she'd told me earlier. *The day he died*, she said and I had assumed she meant after she already knew he was dead.

Jeena nodded tightly. "My wedding dresses. My designs. All those beautiful ideas he had criticised to death. He spent so many years crushing me, making me look small and then he — and that woman. They stole it all without a single thought of what it meant to me."

Quietly, I handed one of the sketch books over to Rosenthal, open to one of the nastier pages of commentary.

"The notes are by Ethan Brady. Jeena was the original designer."

Morgaine and Paisley gasped as if they hadn't been listening in, when Jeena and I first discussed this. Trace handed around a tray of popcorn cauliflower.

"You wanted revenge," Inspector Rosenthal remarked, a leading question if ever there was one. I gave him a disapproving look.

"I did," Jeena breathed. "I wanted to hurt him."

"Did you go for a drive that night?"

She laughed. "No, Inspector. I did not go for a *drive*. I went down to the lounge where Gavin — my father-in-law — was watching television. And I took my dress off."

No one said a word. No one breathed.

"Gavin likes to think he owns everything he pays for," Jeena went on, sounding brittle. "He'd made it very clear for years that I was included in that. Touches that lasted too long, Staring at me, when Ethan was out of the room. Jokes about sharing everything with his son — sometimes when Ethan was right there, not that he'd have done anything. Gavin's sons have never been able to stand up to him. I — well, I managed him. I always have. I kept him at arm's length for as long as I could. On that night, I decided to stop doing that."

Inspector Rosenthal cleared his throat. "So you have an alibi for that evening? You and Gavin Brady?"

Jeena smiled brightly. "Oh, yes. We were together the whole night. First in the lounge room, then in the master bedroom. The original master bedroom. I fully expected Ethan to come back and find us, but he didn't. We got the call at six in the morning that he had been found."

"You were in each other's company the entire time?" the Inspector pressed.

Jeena paused. "Not the entire time. Someone rang the doorbell while we were occupied in the lounge room. I thought perhaps Ethan had left his house key.I went to answer it, wearing nothing but Gavin's shirt."

You had to hand it to her, when she decided on vengeance she went all-out. A jury would hate her.

"Who was at the door?" the Inspector asked.

"Her name's Meegan, isn't it?" Jeena said, as if she didn't know full well who Meegan Kelly was. "He'd mentioned her a few times, as a *friend*." She poured a life-time of distaste into the last word in that sentence. "And there she was on my doorstep. With her $60,000 mint-green electric Mini parked in my driveway. Which answered a lot of questions."

"What did she want?" the Inspector asked.

Jeena's smile went, if possible, colder. "She pretended to be delivering something. She had a garment bag. All innocent. But as soon as I saw the car, I knew they weren't just friends. Naturally she assumed from my state of undress, that I had been with my husband. She tried to hide her feelings. And — well, I was rather cruel to her."

"Cruel how?" Trace asked, clearly as fascinated as the rest of us. The Inspector gave her the dirty look this time, and she mimed zipping her lips.

Jeena took a deep breath. She was calm and clear about all the details, as if she had been running them over in her head, preparing for this moment. "I told her that I knew about the dresses, I had always known, and if she thought she was getting the credit for them, she was mistaken. I also implied that there was a lot more money changing hands than had been spent on her trashy little car, and that Ethan and I laughed about it behind her back. I was, you understand, humiliated. I wanted to make her feel a fraction of what I was feeling."

"What happened next?" asked the Inspector.

"She got so angry," said Jeena, falling back on her old wide-eyed mean girl act. "Furious. She said — something about how he would have Tania over his dead body and drove off in a huff. I don't know what she meant by that, or who Tania was. I didn't care."

"Do you think maybe she said *Titania*?" I interrupted. "It's the name of a dress. She had the Titania in a garment bag right there?"

Inspector Rosenthal coughed disapprovingly at me, as if this wasn't the most important piece of evidence under discussion right now. Meegan had Colette Cray's dress! Where was it now?

"I wasn't really interested," Jeena said. She stared at her lap, her bravado fading a little. "I marched inside, dragged Gavin up to bed and… well. We were busy for a while, then fell asleep. Until the phone call about Ethan."

"You didn't suspect at the time that Meegan might have been the person behind the hit-and-run?" Somehow the Inspector managed to sound entirely un-judgemental.

"I didn't think about that," Jeena insisted. I wasn't sure if I believed her on that one, but she sounded like she believed herself. "I'd told him and Gavin for years how dangerous it was, running on country roads like that. Donovan had tried to tell them, too. Stupid. Asking for trouble. And your people, the police who interviewed us that day after we IDed him at the hospital. They assumed it was an accident right away. I was feeling — well. Guilty. There were a lot of things I chose not to think about."

The Inspector set his notebook aside. "You realise that all this makes it look as if you have a substantial motive for killing Meegan Kelly?"

"Yes," Jeena said tightly. "I am aware. I told Samantha that. She seemed to think you should be informed anyway."

He looked at me. I made an awkward expression in his direction, somewhere between a smile and a shrug.

Maybe Jeena would be lucky. Maybe the jury would be full of women whose husbands had done the dirty on them, who would sympathise with her.

But chances were high that everyone would think she was guilty. And I was the one who insisted she tell the police.

Time would tell whether I had given her very bad advice. Nothing I could do about it now.

Nothing, but find Meegan Kelly's car and the dress that might still be sitting on her back seat.

19

It was a quiet but weird sort of morning at Aunt Harriet's house. Trace was up early to get Daisy ready for school, then headed off for 'brunch with a friend' which I was pretty sure was code for her long-awaited date with Detective Inspector Rosenthal.

Jeena was sleeping on our couch, swaddled in layers of hand-quilted coziness, with a crocheted granny blanket tucked around her feet.

I was supposed to work at the shop this morning, but not to open, which meant I could amble in sometime between nine-thirty and ten. Have I mentioned how much I love my job?

I ate some leftover spinach puffs and drank a cup of peppermint tea before I opened my front door to face the day… and found a handsome man in a good suit leaning against Aunt Harriet's picket fence, carrying a latte in each hand.

Definitely worse ways to start a work day.

"No beach jogging?" I asked Donovan as I accepted

the coffee and fell into step beside him. I wanted to take Victoria Street instead of the main road around to the beach strip, not just because it was a nicer walk (so leafy and pleasant, usually my favourite route) but because I wanted to have a bit of a nose around all the little side streets on my way.

Meegan had travelled separately to her friends, the day she came out here to watch the fashion shoot. Since Leon and Harper still thought Megan was short of money, it made sense she'd been hiding her sporty little brand-new electric Mini from her friends. I was convinced that Leon, at least, knew about Chameleon, but he might have asked a lot of pointed questions if he knew how much money she and E.J. had spent on a fancy car instead of paying the Swoosh Hutch bills.

That day, heaps of cars had been jammed into suburban street parking around here because *Impeccable Magazine* had blocked off their usual parking spots. And Meegan never drove away because she ended up in my bathtub.

So, maybe her car was still here. The police wouldn't have been looking for that specific vehicle before Jeena told Rosenthal it existed. If it was Meegan, not Jeena, who hit Ethan with her car, then surely there had to be some evidence on it. Not to mention the last piece of the Chameleon puzzle: the real Titania dress.

(The one that would prove Vivi was a fraud... if I could get up the nerve to expose her.)

"Colette's at some saltwater spa all day," said Donovan, sounding oddly tense for someone on his day off. "Preparing for her week-long pre-wedding private musical festival bachelorette party. Technically, I'm only her security when she's on business that overlaps with *Impeccable Magazine*. She has her own security team for…"

"Pedicures and hot rock massage?"

"Exactly."

I sipped my latte, covertly checking the driveways as we strolled along Victoria Street. There were a lot of cars parked in the narrow streets around here, as the driveways were tiny.

When we passed Windsor Street, I hung back slightly so Donovan didn't see me looking both ways, up and down. If I didn't spot anything on the way to work, I'd spread my net further after my shift ended, maybe let Paisley in on my theory so we could cover more ground.

Donovan was talking about something, but I was so busy being covert, I'd tuned him out. "Sorry?"

"Jeena," he said, giving me a long look. "No one knows where she is. She didn't come home after the police released her yesterday."

Home, with all its staircases, glass surfaces, sharp corners, and a father-in-law who liked to help himself. I could see why Jeena wasn't keen to head back there, after everything she'd told us. It was possible we had a new housemate now. Once you gave in to Aunt Harriet's cozy layers, it was all over.

"Do you think she did it?" I asked Donovan.

He pushed up his giant sunglasses and stared at me. "Do *you* think she did it? I know you're not Jeena's biggest fan."

"No, that would be Jeena," I said automatically. It's so easy to be mean when you have someone pegged as the mean girl for life.

Donovan gave a short laugh. "No, that would be my dad. To hear him talk, she's the best thing since electric cars. He likes her better than his actual kids."

I managed to control my face so I couldn't reveal how grossed out I was by how much Gavin Brady liked his daughter-in-law.

My phone buzzed and I checked it quickly for a text from Trace:

R reckons they won't arrest J until they find M's car to prove her story

Police doing the rounds of M's friends + relatives today

I texted back quickly:

Does he know you're pumping him for info?

She replied:

Shut up, still the best date in ages. Sips macchiato.

Donovan looked amused. "Something going on?"

"My sister's on her first date in five decades, we're very excited for her."

I wasn't sure what I should be doing. Did I want to make it easier for Rosenthal to arrest Jeena? I believed she hadn't killed Meegan. If I found the car, I'd have to tell the police, and she'd get arrested faster.

Or maybe not. Maybe they still needed more evidence. One thing I'd learned during my time as a prime suspect (and later, as the accused in a court case) was that police like to have all their T's crossed and I's dotted before they show their hand. If the washing machine evidence was enough to bring Jeena in under formal arrest, they'd have done it already.

Who else could have used that washing machine anyway? Various staff members at the house, Donovan, of course — though he'd been with me when Meegan was killed. Gavin Brady? Could he have killed Meegan and driven like a bat out of hell to fetch Donovan from the Swoosh Hutch straight afterwards? He had even more motive than Jeena to go after Ethan's killer, and he'd been there that night. He had to know Meegan was a likely suspect for that hit and run.

Ugh, no. *Stop trying to solve the murder, Sam.* This part wasn't my job. The police would find the car soon enough, and Jeena would or would not be arrested, and I couldn't make a difference to the outcome either way.

The dress, though. There was still a chance that the real, the original Titania gown was somewhere in that car. And it did not deserve to disappear into an evidence locker for the next six months, even if Vivi Wave had tricked Colette Cray into thinking her new one was just as good.

I was so busy wondering what I should do if I found the damned car, I almost missed it. I peered around at the last minute as we passed Albert Street, caught a corner of mint green sticking out from behind a battered Volvo, tripped over my shoes and almost face-planted into Donovan's side.

He was remarkably solid. He was also laughing. "Are you all right there? You're barely with me today."

I had to decide whether or not to trust him. The police would eventually figure out that this was a place they should be looking.

I really wanted to find that dress, though it was Donovan's quest more than mine. I wasn't about to blurt out Jeena's story or her whereabouts — if she wanted to steer clear of the entire Brady family, I was 100% Team Jeena. But for this, he could be useful.

"I think I've just seen Meegan Kelly's car," I admitted.

Donovan straightened up, his serious face dropping into place. The professional security man, all business. Weirdly reassuring. "Show me."

(He didn't say 'what car.')

I led the way into the side street — a cul-de-sac, with only a few houses, and even more cars, lined up along an unsealed pavement. A ute, a Volvo, a couple of clunkers, and then this shiny piece of beautiful hardware.

Donovan gave the car a hard look, then back at me. "*Meegan's* car. Are you sure? These things cost a bomb."

"Sticker price of $60,000 at Brady's Electric Dreams," I said with a flourish. "That's where your brother put the money that was paid to him by *Impeccable Magazine*, and Colette Cray's people. He must not have given himself a discount, but I guess he got the sales percentage."

Donovan swore, and circled the car like an angry car yard customer looking for a flaw. "*Seriously*?"

"Seriously."

Around the front of the car, he stopped moving, then crouched low, one hand outstretched. "There's a dent here."

I winced. "Thought there might be."

He rocked back on his heels. "Meegan —"

Jeena didn't need another person coming after her for killing Meegan, but on the other hand, it would suck to be the only member of the Brady family who didn't know what was going on.

"She was at the house, the night your brother died," I said. "The police know that, and it looks like Meegan was responsible for what happened to Ethan. A dent in the front of the car will probably help them prove it."

Donovan was very still, thoughtful. "No way my dad didn't know Ethan bought that car. And right under Jeena's nose! What the hell was he thinking?"

My phone buzzed with a couple more texts from Trace, but I ignored them. I didn't need updates on the quality of her Eggs Benedict, or her thinking process around dating a police inspector old enough to be her... significantly older boyfriend.

"Your dad probably just thought Ethan was, you know. Buying a car for his girlfriend. Do people say mistress these days? Bit on the side. All those demeaning terms."

Donovan circled the car again. "He probably cheered Ethan on," he muttered, then gave me a sharp look. "He loved that kind of talk. All men together. He has all these sexist rules for car sales, you know? Always pretend you know male customers from somewhere, they love it, like they're in a special club with you. Makes them want to spend more money. Always pretend you don't recognise women, even returning customers. Reduces their confidence, makes them more compliant."

Gavin Brady, the gift that keeps giving.

Donovan's eyes blazed with something like anger. "How long has Jeena known about this?"

"Can you see anything in the car?" I returned quickly, not wanting to get into what Jeena did and didn't know. "I was kind of hoping the Titania was stuffed between the seats. The real Titania."

Donovan leaned into the car. He kept glancing back at that dent, like he couldn't believe it.

I took the opportunity to check my phone to catch up on the reason it had been buzzing for the last few minutes.

From Trace:

Best bacon

Mmmmm fresh squeezed orange juice

How did Rosenthal feel about her spending half of their first date on her phone? I should count myself lucky she was only sending texts and not photos of her food.

WTF the police never found Meegan's phone

I stared at that last text. How did she — but, no. That couldn't be right. They had to have the phone, to confirm the window of her time of death.

As I was looking at it, a new text buzzed in, again from Trace

---

OMG IDIOTS. They never found her phone at the scene, still don't have it. Where are you???

If Meegan's phone wasn't at the scene, then someone had grabbed it. Presumably her murderer.

Damn it, that made sense. So much sense. Leon said Meegan had texted him too, when she disappeared that afternoon, telling him not to worry about her. What if it wasn't Meegan who sent that text?

It didn't have to be Meegan who uploaded her sad-eyes weeping vid to Instagram, either. Her killer could have left the scene, and uploaded the video later. When they had an alibi.

I looked up from my phone, just in time to see Donovan Brady opening the boot of the mint-green electric Mini.

"How did you do that?" I asked.

"These cars have rubbish security," he said, leaning in to pull out a shining garment bag. The Titania.

He hadn't picked the lock. I knew that. I might have been distracted, but I'd heard the tell-tale bipbip of an electronic key fob.

The murderer took her phone and her keys.

"Good trick, you'll have to teach me that," I said brightly, sending a hasty text to my sister. I needed it to be informative, urgent and practical. What I managed was:

Alsbert stSOS

Giving up on being covert, I hit the call button to her and then held my phone loosely by my side. "Is that the dress? Can I see? No wait, we should take it around to the shop, do a proper unveiling."

"May as well do it here," said Donovan, unzipping the bag. "It's not like it's worth fifty grand any more. Colette has her wedding dress. This one's a waste of our time."

The dress unfurled from the garment bag, a wave of bright white fabric, fluffy layers spiralling outwards.

I was pretty sure I was standing a car-length away from a murderer, and desperately trying to come up with an excuse to get out of his company (late for work, I was literally and actually late for work, I didn't need an excuse, I could walk briskly and I'd be safe, I was like, twenty steps away from the beach road and a couple of dozen witnesses).

Still, I couldn't hold back a gasp as I set eyes the real Titania. She was beautiful. That lightness of touch — Meegan's expert sewing skills, and whatever Ethan brought to the party, I guess. Probably paying for the expensive fabrics and not crushing the dressmaker with critical remarks. I finally saw what those round shaped had been all about in the original design — not sequins or lace cut-outs at all. They were white plastic bottle tops. Layers and layers of them, arranged like they were the most expensive beadwork.

"Recycled materials," said Donovan, shaking his head. "Colette would be all over that."

How was it possible, even now with terror spiking into the back of my brain, that I still liked him?

Handsome men with sad eyes who can't be trusted. Samantha Sullivan, you need a new type.

"I have to go," I blurted out. "I'm late for work. The coffee was great and — we should report the car to the police. I can call from the shop, give you a chance to whisk that dress away. It's Colette's, really."

He gave me a long, steady look. "Sam, are you suggesting I remove evidence from the scene of a crime?"

"You literally just did that."

"Maybe you should take the dress." He held it out to me, inviting me to step closer. "Put it with the other one. Let the pop star choose which frock to wear to her wedding."

It was a lovely dress. But. I was pretty sure this man had drowned Meegan Kelly in a bath. He was a big, solid wall of muscle in a nice suit. I was not stepping closer to him, even to make it look like I wasn't suspicious.

"I really have to go. And I'd rather not participate in a — fashion crime. Before lunch. Trying to give them up."

He quirked his eyebrows at me, like I was the only one not acting normal. Was I massively overreacting?

Then he said, very calmly, "You know, don't you."

And just like that, I wasn't wondering whether I was in trouble. I knew it.

20

I HAVE ONE OF THOSE FACES.

People like to tell me things. Little old ladies on the bus always tell me about which of their grandchildren I could date. The mums at Daisy's school take one look at my (apparently) kind eyes, and start massively over-sharing about their love lives and/or the latest erotic romance they've picked for book club.

Bartenders tell *me* what's getting them down.

And, apparently, Donovan Brady wanted to confess his sins.

I can't say I wasn't curious. I had to keep him calm, right? Until someone else turned up. Maybe a neighbour would pop out to tell us to shut up. Maybe Trace had sounded the alert to the local police — I didn't dare look, but as far as I knew, we were still connected by a phone call. Maybe Morgaine would stroll past on her way to work. Maybe…

Maybe I could bite the bullet and start running. He was holding an incredibly expensive wedding dress. That might slow him down. I still had half a mostly-warm latte in a takeaway cup. Maybe I could throw it at him… but no, I couldn't risk the dress.

Maybe I could listen to him bare his soul for a few minutes, and come up with a better plan.

"I don't know anything," I said, sounding a lot more calm than I felt. "You asked me to help." Used me, more like. To make his job easier, at first, and then later, to be his actual alibi. I'd trotted along with it, why? Because I had a crush on him in high school, and he didn't remember me.

Oh hell, he'd used his dad's trick on me, hadn't he? Pretend all men are your best friend, pretend women don't matter. I'd fallen for it.

"This bloody dress," Donovan growled, shaking the garment bag. "Last week, all I wanted was to find it. If *Impeccable* pulls their accounts from Brick Wall Security, my business goes under. There was no way I was going to admit to my dad that I'd failed."

"You didn't fail," I assured him. Calm and steady.

Soothing people was a huge part of my job, back when I was a wedding planner. Grooms fell into two types: baffled shadows who didn't care what happened on the big day, and repressed groomzillas just waiting to bust out emotions about the wrong shade of Bentley, or some relative who definitely shouldn't be invited because of what he said about Our Sharon.

The cliché tells you that brides and their mothers melt down on the big day, but I'd talked so many grooms off the ledge it wasn't even funny. Not to mention their dads!

Do you know how many absent, toxic fathers still

expect to be invited to a wedding, even if they haven't had
a civil conversation with their kids in years? Not to
mention all the stepfathers and groom's fathers, who pays
for what, who dances with the bride, who walks down the
aisle. All ego and feelings.

Weddings. So much pressure. It's amazing I lasted in
that industry as long as I did. But it taught me a few
survival skills.

I was using my gentlest 'everything's going to be all
right' voice right now, as I observed Donovan Brady. He
looked agitated, tense. With any luck I could direct his
energy into guilty sobs instead of smashing my head
against a fence post. With any luck.

"You found the dress," I said softly. "Take the win.
You did great."

"After it didn't matter any more."

"Colette's fine, she's not going anywhere. *Impeccable*
are happy with the photo shoot. It all worked out."

His hands tensed on the gown, squeezing handfuls of
the white fabric. "It was here the whole time," he
muttered. "A block away. She could have just *told* me she
had it."

"You mean Meegan."

"She laughed at me." Donovan looked faraway, as
if he honestly hadn't been thinking about this until
now — like the memory came as a surprise. I
suppose if I had an aggressive dad always shouting
me down, I'd be really good at compartmentalising
too. "She was high. Thought she was hilarious. Said
the dress was going to make her rich and famous.
Some shit about Ethan I didn't even understand at the

time — about how he was trying to cut her out of the deal."

That was Jeena's fault, stirring the pot. But the rest of it… oh. A tragedy all around.

"Did you know?" I asked. "That Meegan and Ethan were working together as Chameleon?"

"I thought it was just her. He was the agent. She was the designer. She was in my way. I wasn't going to hurt her, I was just — trying to get her to calm down. Tell me where she'd stashed the dress." He sounded reasonable. If he kept up this tone and his big sad eyes, a jury would probably be on his side… to a point.

"Did you break open the laundry?" Since I was stuck here, I might as well get all my answers. More efficient than taking a police inspector to brunch. If I could keep Donovan talking long enough… maybe Trace would hear what was being said. Maybe she understood my messed-up text. I could really do with a rescue.

Donovan's face creased up. "No, that was *her*. She wouldn't answer my questions in front of her friends. When I saw her sneak around your shop on her own, it was my chance. I saw the tail end of her filming her stupid video. I told her to delete it, and she laughed at me."

Clearly, not a man who was used to being laughed at.

"So, Meegan broke the laundry door?"

"With a brick." He shook the dress in frustration. "She wanted the other dresses. Reckoned she was owed them. Saying all this crazy stuff. About fashion and money and cars, and Ethan. Maybe she thought I was Ethan for a while there. I don't know what she was on."

Something recreational, clearly. The police must know

what she'd taken. It probably didn't matter now. "Meegan admitted she hit Ethan with her car?"

"*No*," Donovan said, looking horrified. "She blamed Jeena for that. She said it was *Jeena*. She was going to tell everyone. Waving her phone around. The truth will be heard, or whatever."

"You believed her." Everyone always believes the worst of Jeena.

"Meegan had something on that phone that was going to hurt my family," Donovan said fiercely. "I tried to get it off her, that's all. But she ran into the laundry shed, hissed at me like a cat. *Bitch*."

Nothing like the word 'bitch' in the mouth of a man to make him less attractive.

I raised my eyebrows. "Are you saying Meegan tripped and fell into the bath?"

Donovan smiled. Not a pleasant smile. "I should tell the police that. You know what they're like. Give them a believable story, and you can get away with anything. Isn't that what you did?"

Outrage rose in my chest. Seriously not the time. But wow, I was glad I had never got around to making out with his face. High school crush, officially over. Closure achieved.

"What's the real story?"

Donovan's face was cold. All that warmth and humour I'd seen before, in between the sad eyes. Had he been faking that? Was it that easiy to switch it on and off? "She was backed up in the corner, trying to send her stupid little video. I wanted to scare her. Grabbed her legs."

I could imagine that. He was strong; a sudden movement. Down she went. Head under water, impossible to get to air, not without his help.

There was a famous murderer once who did that to a whole series of his brides, and got away with it for ages because he kept changing his name, and they didn't have the internet yet. If it happened today, he'd have been caught by a true crime podcast.

"The phone didn't even go underwater," Donovan said. "And later, when I looked at the video — she'd set it up ready to post, hadn't hit send. It didn't even say anything all that incriminating."

"So, you sent it." I'd figured out that much. "When you were in the car with me, maybe? Or at the Swoosh Hutch? To set up an alibi, so no one would suspect you." It was getting harder to stay soothing and neutral, to not tip him off that I thought he was a monster. "You probably could have got someone to resuscitate her. If you'd called for an ambulance straight away. You could have tried."

"I know," said Donovan Brady. He looked down at the bright white wedding dress in his hands. "Ethan really made this?"

"I don't think so." I had to drag this out. I didn't know what was going to happen if he stopped talking. "Meegan must have made it. Ethan stole the designs from Jeena."

Donovan's face cleared, like that made sense to him. "Is that why Jeena killed him?"

I blinked. Clearly I wasn't the worst fashion detective, of the two of us. "You literally just saw the dent in Meegan's car. You still think Jeena… is that why you tried to frame Jeena with the shirt?"

Donovan wasn't wearing a white shirt that day. Tight

black t-shirt. Meegan wore a shirt, though. I remembered the sight of her on the beach, with it fluttering around her. It was gone later, when she filmed her video. Ethan's killer parading around in his old clothes? She couldn't have been more obvious if she'd tried, and yet no one suspected her.

Maybe if I'd paid more attention to her clothes, I would have figured this out earlier.

"Were you even wearing it when you drowned her?" I accused. "Or did you splash it later, after she was dead, to make Jeena look guilty?" That might explain why there were no tell tale green dye marks on his arms. He could even have worn gloves, to be extra careful.

I felt vindicated in my theory that Jeena would never have gone near a dye bath while wearing a white Prada dress.

Donovan turned on me, approaching in a slow stride, like he'd just realised I was a danger to him.

"They'll go easy on you," I said hastily. "You were under stress. You can afford good lawyers, or your dad can."

I wasn't wrong. It would be easy for the media to spin this so Donovan (attractive white man, everything to live for) was the victim, and Meegan the heartless woman who caused all the drama.

(Except that I knew too much, didn't I? They'd call me as a witness for the bloody prosecution.)

Donovan's muscles bunched. His whole body convulsed, and he tore the wedding dress right down the middle. Bottle tops sprang free. Highly expensive fabric screamed apart with a violent ripping sound.

And then he came for me.

A wedding planner has to be put together. Good clothes, expert makeup. That's how you sell your client the idea that you can achieve perfection on their big day, before you even open your mouth.

I was good at it: the nails, the eyes, the heels. A perfect blend of foundation, shaped hair and confident smile.

Did I mention the heels?

No one cared what I wore at Fashionably Late. Shirt and jeans, mostly. I was starting to play a little with colours and jewellery, the occasional interesting jacket or scarf I fell in love with in the shop. Nothing that compared with the dramatic looks shaped by Paisley and Morgaine and Diana. Half the time I was on laundry duty anyway. Why bother?

"Wear what you like," Morgaine said, my first day. "But wear comfortable shoes."

If I'd uncovered a murderer during my wedding planner days, I probably wouldn't have been able to outrun him.

I didn't outrun him this time. Not even in the world's comfiest sneakers and oldest jeans. But I ran. I tore around the corner block and a half, pulse racing, breath burning my throat, then managed one more corner before Donovan Brady's weight slammed into me from behind, crashing us both to the pavement.

A sharp whistle tore through the air.

I'd made it. The rough concrete stinging my palms was the pavement on the beach road. The shopping stretch. Within sight of Fashionably Late.

There were people around us. The beach road is never empty. People staring from their cars, and across the road with dogs on leashes. There, halfway down the street between us and the shop was Paisley. Their was phone pointed at us. Recording.

Donovan's weight on my back lessened slightly as he realised he was being observed.

"Smile," yelled Paisley, trying to sound confident. "This is going out to all twelve of my subscribers."

The pressure eased. I scrambled away from him, moving to stand beside Paisley. Not that they'd be a lot of protection against Mr Brick Wall, but at least I wasn't being filmed any more.

Donovan looked stunned, like he was the one who had been slammed into the ground. He had no idea what to do next.

That made two of us.

"You should talk to your sister," Paisley advised me.

I reached into my pocket and pulled out the phone. Miraculously, the call between us hadn't cut out. "Trace?"

"*Sam*! We're eight minutes away. I'm never going to brunch again. You can't be trusted on your own."

"Police are here," I said, mouth dry. "No worries." Clearly, phone calls had been made. A police car rolled along the beach road, lights flashing lazily, no siren. They parked near us. Two officers inside, and I didn't know them.

"Are you going to be okay?" my sister asked, knowing that a police presence was the opposite of reassuring, where I was concerned.

"Samantha," said Inspector Rosenthal to me, from

Trace's phone. "Give them your phone. I'll talk to the officers."

Donovan Brady still hadn't got up. He leaned back against a concrete fence, looking wrecked.

"It's okay," I said into the phone. "I can handle it."

21

COLETTE CRAY WAS MARRIED A WEEK AND A HALF LATER, at a secret location somewhere in southern Tasmania. I hear the guest list was so restricted, only half the cast of *Home and Away* got invited.

I don't know all the details — the latest issue of *Impeccable Magazine* hasn't yet hit the stands, with its exclusive photos — but rumour has it the celebration included authentic Mongolian yurts, a three day tasting banquet of Huon Valley produce, a rustic open-air dancing pavilion, a bonfire in which they symbolically burned a specially-commissioned art installation representing World Hunger, and countless photo opportunities with baby goats.

Just your average Tassie bush party. But the celebs had had a nice time, or so they all claimed once they recovered from the social media blackout.

Along with the rest of the Fashionably Late crew, I was invited to completely different exclusive party, a couple of weeks after the wedding, where Vivi Wave and Jeena Harding (she dropped the hyphen-Brady so fast you'd think it was last year's eyeliner) announced their new business venture, Chameleon Couture.

They'd decided between themselves that sharing the identity of Chameleon made for a better narrative than Jeena exposing Vivi's lie — and of course, Vivi brought her fashion industry experience and established boutique to the new business venture, while Jeena brought piles of cash and her innovative designs.

They held the party at the Swoosh Hutch, which also benefited from a new injection of Jeena's cash — she signed up for her own studio membership, and covered the repair bills to the landlord.

Harper and Leon were treating her like she was their saviour and new best friend. Chameleon Couture had a lot to offer them both.

Gavin Brady closed all four of his car yards on the day his son Donovan was arrested for the murder of Meegan Kelly, and no one had seen him in public for weeks. His ads were pulled. His business website disappeared. Without Gavin putting pressure on the landlord, and with the fierce, wealthy Jeena Harding in their corner, the Swoosh Hutch gang had managed to hang on to their precious makerspace by their fingernails.

The safe money was on Brady rebranding the yards, soft-launching back into the public eye under another name, and keeping himself distant from the new brand as long as it kept bringing in the cash. Electric cars were a hot commodity and someone had to sell them.

Jeena was planning to send herself to design school to develop the skills she'd always wanted, but she saw no need to hold back from starting the business with Vivi straight away, especially with the triumph of the Titania about to hit the public eye thanks to *Impeccable Magazine*.

I gave Jeena a few lessons how to dye fabric, when we worked together on the 'staging' of Colette's wedding dress. Purple and green on the under layers. In honour of the horrific end of the original Titania, we ripped the top skirt into ribbons so the colour showed through. We even added a layer of bottle tops, since that was the one thing that Colette Cray liked better about the first version.

Colette looked like a fairy princess at her final gown fitting, which was exactly what we'd been going for. I'd already received twelve orders for wedding veils featuring my signature 'ripped and dyed' style. Fashionably Late were doing just fine out of our own collaboration with Chameleon Couture.

Trace brought Inspector Rosenthal as her date to the Swoosh Hutch party. He wore the ugliest suit I've ever seen in my life. I'm still not sure if he chose it deliberately, in a genius attempt to troll the fashionistas of Hobart, or if it's actually his only suit. I haven't told him yet that the candid shots from the party turned him into a surprise Instagram icon. I'll wait until he has a mouthful of coffee or something.

Diana Wave made a rare public appearance at the party, graciously endorsing her daughter Vivi's success, and generally being stylish and hilarious.

At one point, she swept past me with the world's largest glass of sparkling white (I swear she must have brought the glass with her, as everyone else was drinking out of mason jars) and said "Well done, Sam. I knew you'd fit in well with our Fashionably Late family."

I was on my third drink and feeling brave, so I blurted out: "Why did you take the chance on me, when I applied for the job? I know you had a lot of applicants."

Diana gave me one of her patented superior expressions, all poised and twinkling. "I find that people who have been through hell are the most interesting people to know," she said airily. "Also, I liked your face."

"Eventually," remarked Paisley, as Diana wafted away again, "You learn not to ask her those sort of questions."

"How else would I end up in super awkward conversations? Awkward conversations are my best thing."

"I'd disagree with you," said Paisley. "But it might get awkward."

Somehow, as the party with all its luvvie-darlingness and arty cleverness began to wind down, I found myself once again ambling through the old church, with its internal studio walls.

The Space Harpy studio space looked much the same, maybe with a bit more glitter than usual.

I walked over to the empty studio that had belonged to Meegan, and for a moment imagined myself being good enough one day to work here, to have my own dress designs pinned up on a wall.

(Not while Jeena was in the group, obviously. I could cope with us being sort-of friends now, but I was relieved when she abandoned Aunt Harriet's quilted sofa to take back possession of her marital home. Sharing a workspace with her might lead to a whole different murder scenario.)

Jeena's studio space was the third corner, the one that had originally belonged to Ethan "E.J." Brady. She'd redrawn a lot of her old sketches, larger and on quality paper, so she could look at the designs without seeing the horrendous critiques of her gaslighting husband. There were new ones, too. Including fierce splashes of colour that I like to think were inspired by our day of dye training.

Quiet steps echoed behind me, and I turned to see Inspector Rosenthal, holding a plate of tiny quiches and sandwiches, and a bottle of locally sourced organic cider.

"Nice suit," I told him.

"Thank you," he said politely. "Everyone keeps saying that. I assume it's sarcasm?"

"Hard to know, with this crowd." It was odd, being in his company. I didn't feel as desperately stressed by his very existence any more. Was it because I didn't mentally categorise him as 'police' or 'threat' any more, because of seeing him around Trace? Or was I just... adapting to my past trauma? "I don't hate you dating my sister," I told him.

"Thank you," he said again. "I appreciate that."

"Not saying it's not completely weird."

"Right."

"You are not her type at *all*."

"Noted."

"Am I a completely terrible judge of character?" I asked plaintively.

Rosenthal blinked, looking startled. "Are you still talking about me and your sister?"

"No."

He seemed to understand, then. "Am I?" he suggested.

"Are you what?"

"A completely terrible judge of character."

I let out a short laugh. "Well, yes. Sometimes. Under certain circumstances." Me, for example, the time he decided to arrest me. "You've been doing better recently." He'd picked Trace, after all. "Marked improvement."

"Sometimes that's all we can ask for."

"I suppose I'm improving too," I mused. "I only trusted Donovan Brady for like, a week. With Malcolm, it was seven years."

"There you are, then. Where there's room for improvement, there's hope, don't you think?" Inspector Rosenthal looked at me thoughtfully. "You know, you were my first."

"First time you arrested someone who turned out to be innocent?" That seemed unlikely.

"No, definitely not." We shared the world's awkwardest laugh at that. It really wasn't funny. "Yours was the first case," he went on. "The first one where I didn't realise I'd made the wrong call until too late, when the trial was underway. I let assumptions get in the way of evidence. And I was furious at myself."

I looked at him steadily. "That's something, I suppose." I was prepared to accept him as Trace's boyfriend, if that was where they were heading (and I couldn't see her starting anything unless she saw a serious outcome, not with her charts and lists and planning brain). But forgiving and forgetting? That was harder.

"Understanding the mistake I made with you, coming to terms with it," he went on. "It's made me better at my job."

"Glad to be of service." That *was* sarcasm. "And how do you feel about your deep lack of knowledge about social media, modern phone use and fashion?"

"That if it comes up again in future cases, I should consult someone who knows what they're talking about."

I smiled sweetly at him. "Check with Paisley about our hourly rate."

Inspector Rosenthal gave me a slightly hunted look. "You're not actually planning to investigate crimes, are you? Because it really is most unwise for an amateur..."

I patted him comfortingly on the shoulder. "Only fashion crimes, Inspector. Like that suit of yours."

Inspector Rosenthal looked reassured, so I chose not to explain to him about the new sign Paisley had recently posted in the Fashionably Late shop window.

THE FASHION DETECTIVES
WE SOLVE CRIMES CONNECTED TO
CLOTHING, COSTUMES AND COUTURE
REASONABLE RATES, INQUIRE WITHIN.

I'd break it to him later. Much later.
Possibly, when he had a mouthful of coffee.

THE END

*Samantha Sullivan & the Fashionably Late crew will return in Book #2: **Drop Dead in Red**!*

ACKNOWLEDGMENTS

This book was written on *lutruwita* (Tasmania) Aboriginal land. I acknowledge, with deep respect, the traditional owners of this land, the palawa people.

All my love and thanks to the readers and writers of the Terror Australis Festival (TAF Murder She Wrote 2019!) who inspired me, reminding me why I love crime fiction and why it's so important to me to write mysteries set here in Tasmania, at the end of the world.

Huge shout out to my first readers for this book: Isabel, Liz and Katharine, whose feedback was essential.

Thanks to Elizabeth of Earl Grey Editing for her proof-reading services, and to April Anderton of Indie Cover Market for the Fashionably Late cover art.

As ever, I am grateful for the support of my family & friends who continue to rally around me whenever there is

a new book to launch into the world… and don't complain
too much when I disappear to write the next one.

livia day

ABOUT THE AUTHOR

Livia Day lives in Tasmania, an island state of Australia where she plots all her murders.

If you like your dead bodies with a side of cake, you may enjoy the delicious Cafe La Femme series:

- *A Trifle Dead*
- *Drowned Vanilla*
- *Keep Calm and Kill the Chef*

Join Livia's monthly newsletter:
https://mailchi.mp/tansyrr/liviaday

Drop Dead in Red

(Fashionably Late #2)

Iconic, glamorous filmmaker Prudence Scythe went missing fourteen years ago and was never found... until now, when her dead body turns up on a goat farm in rural Tasmania.

Where has she been all this time? Why was she wearing an evening gown in a muddy paddock? Most importantly: where did she get that drop dead gorgeous red dress?

Once again, the Fashionably Late boutique is tangled up with a local murder. It's up to Samantha Sullivan and her friends to investigate, so the wrong person isn't blamed for this crime of fashion.